# Bello:
## hidden talent rediscovered!

Bello is a digital only imprint of Pan Macmillan, established to breathe new life into previously published, classic books.

At Bello we believe in the timeless power of the imagination, of good story, narrative and entertainment and we want to use digital technology to ensure that many more readers can enjoy these books into the future.

We publish in ebook and Print on Demand formats to bring these wonderful books to new audiences.

*About Bello:*
www.panmacmillan.com/imprints/bello

*About the author:*
www.panmacmillan.com/author/royvickers

B E L L O

## Roy Vickers

Roy Vickers was the author of over 60 crime novels and 80 short stories, many written under the pseudonyms Sefton Kyle and David Durham. He was born in 1889 and educated at Charterhouse School, Brasenose College, Oxford, and enrolled as a student of the Middle Temple. He left the University before graduating in order to join the staff of a popular weekly. After two years of journalistic choring, which included a period of crime reporting, he became editor of the *Novel Magazine*, but eventually resigned this post so that he could develop his ideas as a freelancer. His experience in the criminal courts gave him a view of the anatomy of crime which was the mainspring of his novels and short stories. Not primarily interested in the professional crook, he wrote of the normal citizen taken unawares by the latent forces of his own temperament. His attitude to the criminal is sympathetic but unsentimental.

Vickers is best known for his 'Department of Dead Ends' stories which were originally published in *Pearson's Magazine* from 1934. Partial collections were made in 1947, 1949, and 1978, earning him a reputation in both the UK and the US as an accomplished writer of 'inverted mysteries'. He also edited several anthologies for the Crime Writers' Association.

*Roy Vickers*

# SEVEN CHOSE MURDER

BELL○

First published in 1959 by Faber & Faber

This edition published 2012 by Bello
an imprint of Pan Macmillan, a division of Macmillan Publishers Limited
Pan Macmillan, 20 New Wharf Road, London N1 9RR
Basingstoke and Oxford
Associated companies throughout the world

www.panmacmillan.com/imprints/bello
www.curtisbrown.co.uk

ISBN 978-1-4472-2459-4 EPUB
ISBN 978-1-4472-2458-7 POD

Copyright © Roy Vickers 1959

The right of Roy Vickers to be identified as the
author of this work has been asserted in accordance
with the Copyright, Designs and Patents Act 1988.

Every effort has been made to contact the copyright holders of the material reproduced in this book. If any have been inadvertently overlooked, the publisher will be pleased to make restitution at the earliest opportunity.

You may not copy, store, distribute, transmit, reproduce or otherwise make available this publication (or any part of it) in any form, or by any means (electronic, digital, optical, mechanical, photocopying, recording or otherwise), without the prior written permission of the publisher. Any person who does any unauthorized act in relation to this publication may be liable to criminal prosecution and civil claims for damages.

The Macmillan Group has no responsibility for the information provided by any author websites whose address you obtain from this book ('author websites'). The inclusion of author website addresses in this book does not constitute an endorsement by or association with us of such sites or the content, products, advertising or other materials presented on such sites.

This book remains true to the original in every way. Some aspects may appear out-of-date to modern-day readers. Bello makes no apology for this, as to retrospectively change any content would be anachronistic and undermine the authenticity of the original. Bello has no responsibility for the content of the material in this book. The opinions expressed are those of the author and do not constitute an endorsement by, or association with, us of the characterization and content.

A CIP catalogue record for this book is available from the British Library.

Visit **www.panmacmillan.com** to read more about all our books
and to buy them. You will also find features, author interviews and
news of any author events, and you can sign up for e-newsletters
so that you're always first to hear about our new releases.

# Contents

| | |
|---|---|
| Dossier of the Dacey Murders | 1 |
| A Toy for Jiffy | 31 |
| Marion, Come Back | 53 |
| A Woman of Principle | 85 |
| Spinster's Evidence | 113 |
| The Case of Poor Gertrude | 143 |
| No Women Asked | 163 |

# Dossier of the Dacey Murders

# Chapter One

In England the popular press likes its front-page murders to fit into the framework of the old melodramas; Mrs. Dacey, being a second wife, therefore became Julia Dacey's Cruel Stepmother. By the time a studio photograph of this rather stodgy matron had been built up by the staff artists, she really did look preposterously cruel.

Julia, being blue-eyed, attractive, and well-behaved, was cast for the nitwit heroine whose beauty and innocence make her anybody's dupe—until they decided to groom her for the role of The Maniac Killer. William Millard, disappointingly, who appeared to be a steady kind of man, was a very doubtful choice for The Matrimonial Adventurer. But the Dacey home was just what a news editor would have ordered. It was an Eighteenth Century Manor House with a three-acre garden—at Fendlesham, a one-time village some twenty miles out of London.

The Maniac Killer idea had a springboard of fact in a tragic actuality. There was no mystery about it—the family had never tried to hush it up. Julia herself mentioned it to Millard.

Matrimonial Adventurer or not, Millard wanted Julia as Julia, and told her so in the garden after lunch, on his first visit to her home.

"I'm glad you asked me." She was very grave about it. "Before I answer, I'm going to give you a chance to back out. Don't speak, please! When I was seventeen, I killed a girl at school. I was at Hendlemere—up the river, near Thanford. On River days—two a week—senior girls took turns being in charge of the boathouse, with three junior girls—twelve-year-olds—to do the chores, which included checking the paddles and punt cushions.

"Punt cushions!" she repeated. "You know what I mean? They aren't cushions but hard mattresses about half the size of a bed mattress. They were kept in a dark, cavernous sort of cupboard. I threw one in the cupboard, not knowing Doris Trallen was hiding inside to dodge her share of the work. She was a small girl for her age, and the first cushion knocked her down—at least, that's what we supposed. I shouted to the others to hurry up. We threw twenty-two cushions into that cupboard and then I locked the door. Doris was suffocated and—" Julia stopped short. "But you know already?"

"I do. And I'm wondering why you have to hurt yourself all over again when I'm asking you to marry me."

"I hoped you would hear it first from me, Will!"

"Darling, I almost did! I was nineteen when it happened—I read the news reports at the time. I didn't realize the girl was you until about two hours ago. Just before lunch, when I was small-talking with Mrs. Dacey, she said something—I don't know quite what—but it ended 'since Julia was at Hendlemere.' Then it all flashed up. It was a ghastly accident, but surely you've forgotten it by now!"

So one would think. But there were factors which kept the memory green.

"I'd forgotten it more in the first year than I have now. I have dreams—nightmares."

"Dreaming that you're doing it all over again, I suppose?" His sympathy won her confidence.

"Not quite. The dreams aren't about poor Doris. About me. As if I had a jinx. In the dream it's always the moment after—after the killing. Never anybody I know. Often I dream I have killed animals."

"Let me share the nightmares and maybe they'll go away."

The kiss prevented Julia from relating the repercussion on her own family. But Millard heard it a few minutes later from her father.

Arthur Dacey had been a University lecturer in chemistry (the papers made him a professor and endowed him with absent-mindedness). Shortly after his wife's death, when Julia was five, one of his former students invited him to enter the family business—a small firm of manufacturing chemists. In fifteen years Dacey's work on the extended uses of strychnine (The Murder Drug in the case) turned the small firm into a large company. Dacey discovered that he had accumulated a modest fortune. He resigned, added a laboratory to the Manor House, and continued his researches unhampered by a Board of Directors.

Millard interrupted him in a doze in his study—to make a manly little speech, with a peroration on his inability to keep Julia on the scale to which she was accustomed. Mr. Dacey, who was preoccupied, paid little attention.

"Yes, of course. I gathered that Julia was making up her mind. Very pleased, my dear Millard—er—William. But before we accept our new relationship, I have to fulfill a promise to Julia. The fact is that while she was at school—"

"Thank you, sir, she's told me herself," said Millard and added unwisely, "it must have been a pretty grim business for you."

"It was indeed! I went down to the school, expecting to meet the poor child's parents. Only the mother was there. The parents had been divorced and there was a trust in favor of the child only. The family history seemed to make everything worse, if that were possible. Imagine my position. I could devise no means of consoling the poor woman except the obvious one."

But it was not obvious to Millard.

"I married her, William. Mrs. Dacey! The lady you met at lunch."

Millard recorded in his diary that he was shocked. He seems to have been unable to visualize Mr. Dacey's sense of obligation to the dead child's mother. A little later he noted with regret that Julia herself failed to see anything morbid in this marriage, which served the convenience of all parties. She remained on excellent terms with her stepmother. Mrs. Dacey was a competent housekeeper. The two women ran the large house with one daily cleaner, though Julia, who had graduated in chemistry, gave much time to her father as secretary and bottle-washer.

Mrs. Dacey was short and shapeless, with large prominent eyes and a round face which was emphatically dimpled. She was shy by nature and covered it with a professional cheerfulness. On the surface she was a totally unremarkable, inoffensive woman with a tendency to talk about food.

When Millard came out of the study, Maud Dacey was standing at the table in the hall in the act of opening a box of Athene Chocolates (the name was changed after the scandal). She offered him one, but he declined. In a stroll round the garden she recited Julia's virtues, with frequent pauses for the consumption of chocolates.

Again Millard's diary becomes a minor factor. He records that she took him to a remote corner of the garden and showed him an animal cemetery of seven graves of her personal pets. Two dogs, two cats, two marmosets, and a parrot, all of whom had come to a premature end.

*I wasn't really listening until she came to the parrot, which had belonged to her mother. She told me the parrot had been suffocated . . .*

The diary did not say how or why or by whom.

# Chapter Two

The married life of the Millards is very fully documented—that is, for the first two and a half years. It is but small exaggeration to say that Julia could hardly have replaced a broken coffee cup in that period without the police eventually hearing all about it. Yet the outline of it would fit thousands of lively young couples—the kind who would be very happy, if they had a little more money.

Arthur Dacey bought them a small house at Kingbiton, which is six miles Londonwards of Fendlesham. Millard was showing promise in the actuarial department of an insurance company. His salary provided decency and reasonable comforts—but the reasoning had to be flawless. Mr. Dacey seemed to have forgotten that a house is comparatively useless without furniture. So their car was a veteran.

Twice a week Julia would run over to Fendlesham to type and index her father's notes and tidy his laboratory, which the cleaner refused to enter. Maud Dacey had been coached in handling apparatus, with doubtful results. Most of the laboratory chores remained for Julia. In return, Maud would pop in and out of Kingbiton to do little jobs for Julia. After the first six months a routine was established by which the Millards spent alternate weekends at the Manor House. Sometimes Millard would help his wife clean the laboratory. So he had access to the strychnine as easily as Mrs. Dacey and Julia.

The Millards were popular. It always costs a little more to be popular than one thinks. There was much checking of each other's figures.

"*During this two and a half years, Mrs. Millard, would you say that your relations with your husband were harmonious?*"

"*Yes, very harmonious.*"

That was all Julia said. Chief Inspector Curwen never pressed a question. For a complete answer we must skim a dozen pages of the report and weld odd bits together.

"Before we had been married a year, we were always having to talk about money. We didn't accuse each other of extravagance, but we did have differences of opinion."

"For instance?"

"It's hard to give one without being unfair. He said once that my father ought to pay me a salary. I took a degree in chemistry and I act as part-time technical secretary—and bottle-washer-in-chief. I said I would not like to ask my father for a salary because he had made a trust to benefit Mrs. Dacey and myself after his death. We didn't quarrel, but I think we were both a little disillusioned."

"Did you, in fact, ask your father for a salary?"

These indirect questions about their affairs and their personal relations pivoted on the incident of the Pekingese dog—a post-honeymoon gift from Maud Dacey. In that childless home the dog had become a personality, a focus of domestic legend, the hero of many a tall story. One Spring evening, after a dinner and theatre party in London, Julia had to be told that the dog was dead. She had gone straight upstairs to hang up her best coat. When she came down, Millard stopped her in the hall and broke it to her as gently as he could.

Julia behaved as would most women of her kind. She was very distressed and rather incoherent. Soon, she asked:

"Where is he?"

"In the sitting room. I've covered him with the rug. You'd better not go in."

"Why mustn't I see Chiang?"

"Darling, there's no must or mustn't. The nightmares have stopped since we've been married. Don't risk starting them again—don't give yourself a visual image of Chiang lying dead. We've had a lot of fun and happiness with that little fellow. Let that memory have a chance to stay uppermost."

"I won't go in if you don't want me to," she agreed. "I can't understand it. He was in perfect health this afternoon. Maud remarked on it when she came in to do the curtains, just before I left to meet you. Why is he—*dead?*"

"Probably his heredity—they're a very artificial breed and I've heard they often die suddenly." She looked unconvinced. He added, "Tomorrow, before I go to the office, I'll take him to the Central Pets' Clinic for a *post-mortem*. In a couple of days they'll tell us why."

A couple of days later he handed her a typewritten slip, under the Clinic's letterhead.

"You may understand all that—I don't," he said. "The vet told me that it means one of those seizures which we call 'heart failure.'"

Eventually the police pursued the unimportant death of the dog as they pursued the trivial topics of conversation at the Manor House breakfast table the following June.

Taking breakfast were Mrs. Dacey and the Millards—Mr. Dacey never appeared at breakfast even on the routine weekends.

A meandering chatter was cut short by a high-pitched bellow from upstairs. All three jumped up from the table. Millard reached the bathroom first and said that Arthur Dacey had answered him, but too indistinctly. The door was a heavy one and it took Millard a few minutes to break a panel with a footstool.

Arthur Dacey was lying dead. On the floor beside him was a broken tumbler which still held some of his morning saline—and enough strychnine to make a *post-mortem* a purely legal formality.

# Chapter Three

The coroner had been a personal friend. As the procedure is very much what the coroner chooses, the inquest became little more than a funeral oration.

"The police have not invited this court to consider the possibility of foul play," he told his jury. "You may conclude that the strychnine must therefore have been placed in that glass by deceased's own hand. Your task is to decide whether he did so of design or by accident." He was scornful of the possibility of even the most temporary insanity. He drew a picture of an eminent scientist "absorbed in his work," suddenly going down to his laboratory, perhaps with the glass of saline in his hand—and so on. The jury returned a verdict of accidental death.

But the police do not confide their hopes and fears to a coroner's court. Waiting at the Manor House was Chief Inspector Curwen of Scotland Yard, who told Millard that he had come to inspect the laboratory. He broke the seals affixed by the local police and found the laboratory remarkable only for its tidiness.

"Spick-and-span! Looks as if it were kept only for show."

"My wife and I cleaned it on Saturday afternoon. I don't think Mr. Dacey entered it again, although the coroner suggested that he must have." Led by Curwen, Millard described the routine of the house.

"So Mrs. Millard had free access to the laboratory at all times?"

"Everybody had free access. Nominally, the door was kept locked, but the key was always hanging on a hook in the hall."

That, decided Curwen, was practically the end of the case. Nearly all convicted poisoners have been caught through the police linking them with the source of the poison. Here it would be possible to link all the members of the household and most of the dead man's friends.

Julia, after confirming her husband's statements, said that her father made constant use of strychnine in his experiments. She produced laboratory records, which she herself had kept up to date. A few minutes later the fact emerged—checked subsequently by other chemists—that approximately 500 grains of strychnine had been removed since Saturday morning. Curwen was surprised only by the amount.

Maud Dacey, interviewed in the dining room, spoke as if her late husband had been a much respected employer.

"When Julia—Mrs. Millard—first married I used to clean up in the laboratory. I'm afraid I failed to give satisfaction—I think, really, I was afraid of all those poisons lying about."

It was an odd picture of a research chemist at work and Curwen smiled indulgently.

"I don't say I ever *saw* anything like that—only test tubes and things to be washed in a special way. But a lot of those scientific things are invisible, aren't they, and they might cling to your clothes without your knowing it." She added with a sigh, "I shall always believe that was how Chiang met his death."

"Who was Chiang, Mrs. Dacey?"

"We were told it was heart failure, and of course it may have been—oh, Chiang was a Pekingese—the dearest little dog. He was in perfect health. I was the last to see him alive—"

Curwen escaped as soon as politeness permitted. While exchanging small talk with Millard on his way to the car he wondered why Mrs. Dacey had dragged in that silly story about the little dog.

"What did your Pekingese die of, Mr. Millard?"

"Strychnine poisoning." Millard frowned. "It's a pity Mrs. Dacey mentioned it. I know it was strychnine because I had a *post-mortem* on the dog. But that's all I can tell you. I haven't the ghost of a notion how the stuff got into its food."

And nobody had the ghost of a notion how the strychnine had got into Dacey's saline, thought Curwen.

"Mrs. Dacey thinks the dog died of heart failure."

"She does. And so does my wife." Millard groaned. "I do most earnestly request you not to reveal to them what I have told you."

"I can't make any promises."

"That's a pity!" snapped Millard. "A rule like that must often antagonize people who begin by wanting to help you."

"I suppose I asked for it!" grinned Curwen. "We don't tell anybody anything we don't have to tell 'em."

"The examination," said Millard, relenting, "was done by a Mr. Carshaw, of the Central Pets' Clinic, Brandover Street. I told him what I intended to do. He did not exactly consent, but he looked the other way while I pinched a piece of his notepaper to fake a report."

"But why did you have to deceive the ladies?"

"Be human, Inspector. A woman can get very fond of a dog. My wife is imaginative and slightly neurotic. She had free access to that lab. In a fortnight she would have been accusing herself of killing her own dog through some impossible carelessness of her own."

"We'll see how we go," compromised Curwen and turned back to the house, this time to begin a full-dress investigation.

In a couple of months Curwen possessed all the evidence obtainable—and failed to achieve even so much as an inspired guess.

"There could have been a double miracle, sir—one killing the Peke and the other killing the man," he told the Assistant Commissioner. "If miracles are barred, there's Mrs. Dacey and the Millards—one or the lot! If Millard poisoned his wife's dog, why did he pay the vet to tell him so? If Mrs. Dacey poisoned the dog while she was alone in the house that evening, why offer me the dog story?"

"I know how you feel, Curwen." His chief was not wholly

convinced that there had even been a crime. "But you can't altogether rule out coincidence."

"Just so, sir!" Curwen was nothing if not respectful. "And I can't rule out nearly five hundred grains of strychnine missing from the old man's stock. That's an ounce, and it would go into a small phial. The dog and the man between 'em had ten grains—which is nearly ten times the fatal dose."

Curwen came to his final grievance.

"It isn't as though any of 'em had a police record for us to work on!"

None of them had a police record. But the Assistant Commissioner's daughter was the same age as Julia and had been at the same school at the time Doris Trallen had met her death. But he did not mention it to Curwen because, being a sensible man, he considered it irrelevant.

Julia's mourning for her father was bedraggled by the long police investigation. Millard good-temperedly endured frequent heckling on the incident of the Pekingese.

"Your wife left Mrs. Dacey in your house at about six thirty, to join you in London. Mrs. Dacey was back home in the Manor House by eight fifteen. Do you believe that some person unknown broke into your house for the sole purpose of poisoning your dog?"

"Fantastic, of course," agreed Millard. "But when you pin it down like that—where do we go from there?"

Nowhere, admitted Curwen to himself. Assume that poison had been put in the dog's food by Mrs. Dacey—or by Mrs. Millard—or thrust down its throat by Millard before his wife came downstairs. Assume any theory you like, and it still didn't make sense.

# Chapter Four

In deference to Julia's bereavement, Millard restrained his own elation at the change in their circumstances. Julia would benefit by about a thousand pounds a year, which would be doubled on Maud's death. In the meantime, Julia's health was suffering. She admitted that the dreams were returning, with a new twist. It was Maud Dacey who suggested that the Millards should sell their house and share the Manor House with her. ("It's so big that we shan't have to live in each other's pockets.")

Domestically, the arrangement was successful. Julia's health improved. In a few months they had settled into the routine which lasted nearly two years. The Millards acquired their own circle of young couples and gave their own parties, at which Maud would put in a token appearance.

Julia—seen through the eyes of acquaintances during this period—was indistinguishable from any other attractive young wife who is satisfied with her lot. She could keep her end up at a party, without reminding anybody of tragedy in her past. Nobody could point to any sinister characteristic.

Maud Dacey emerges as a placatory figure, with a juvenile appetite for chocolates. Indeed, through all this normality the Athene Chocolates kept bobbing up—a theme song of disaster—involving Millard himself. There were occasions when Maud's cheerful little aphorisms over the evening meal would exasperate him into snarling at her. The following evening he would present her with a box of Athene Chocolates, indistinguishable from those with which she kept herself supplied, which he would buy from the Korner House near his office. He made light of Julia's frequent protests that it was wrong to encourage Maud to exceed the ration imposed by Dr. Blagrove.

One day, a month exactly before the regime came to an abrupt end, Maud called unexpectedly at Millard's office.

"I have heard from my first husband," she told him. "I am afraid he has made no more of a success of his second marriage than of his first. He is now a very lonely man." She sighed. "I admit that in his first marriage there were faults on both sides. We are none of us perfect, and—"

"And he wants you back?" Millard tried to say it naturally.

"Reading between the lines," said Maud, "your guess is probably correct. But the letter is actually from a solicitor and it only asks me to send him—by post—some photographs of our daughter. Doris would have been twenty-one next month, had she lived."

The photos and other mementos were stored with a Safe Deposit company. Millard drove her there and brought the deed-box home—incidentally observing that the account stood in her former name of Trallen.

That night in her bedroom she unlocked the deed-box and reexamined the contents, which had been collected and deposited the day after Arthur Dacey had offered her marriage.

An open box of Athene Chocolates within arm's reach, she took out and handled the objects, which were exclusively personal. Underneath three framed photographs of Doris as a baby and toddler was a packet of snapshots. She lingered over the first half dozen, skimmed the rest, and repacked them all for mailing to the child's father. A lock of hair enclosed in glass; a number of small toys; a jeweler's case; a tiny pair of shoes; some juvenile drawings—the sentimental litter of a woman who had never attempted to understand herself, all undisturbed, unthought of, since her second marriage.

True, a few tears fell. Whether or not any deep feeling for her dead child survived—whether or not she was working up a sentimentalism for a very special purpose—her reaction to the child's trinkets is seen now as a prelude for The Fatal Supper Party—a traditional headline in this type of murder.

In fact, it was not a party, and it wasn't even supper—being the routine evening meal remarkable at the time only for Maud's social and even ethical stupidity.

To begin with, the dress she wore appeared as a joke in bad taste. It was expensive, gay, and designed for a much younger woman. It carried a brooch of singular inappropriateness—an elaborate design of two butterflies, in diamond points and turquoise. Maud herself was self-conscious and fluttery. The Millards exchanged puzzled glances.

"How nice you look, dear!" said Julia. "I've never seen that brooch before—it's intriguing!"

"Today is an anniversary," Maud said. Her round, prominent eyes looked like glass counterfeits. "Today would have been my daughter's twenty-first birthday—if she had lived."

That threw the Millards completely off their balance. Never before had Maud made any allusion to the childhood accident.

"I wouldn't have mentioned it, only it seems foolish to make a bogey of something that happened so long ago—disloyal to our friendship." She beamed on Julia. "This brooch was given to Doris by her uncle when she left home for her first term. Rather unsuitable, really, for a schoolgirl. She never wore it. But she would have worn it today."

Julia achieved a smile. Millard thought that his wife was more puzzled than shocked. Maud's chatter glided into the trivialities of the day. Later, when Julia was pouring the coffee, Maud took from the sideboard a box of Athene Chocolates, removed the cellophane and dropped it in the wastebasket.

"Will has been spoiling me again!" she gushed. "He says he was rude to me this morning, but that's an excuse. You must help me do justice."

Word for word it was the same little speech, made every time she received the placatory gift of chocolates. She held out the open box. Millard reached forward to pass it to Julia. Thus he could not do otherwise than present the opposite end of the box. Julia took a chocolate from the end of the row nearest her hand. Millard then returned the box to Maud.

"I know it's no use trying to press you," she simpered. She took a chocolate herself from the middle of the layer, then replaced the lid. "I shall leave the box on the sideboard, Julia, and I hope you will help yourself."

The Millards had no social engagement, so the two women did the washing-up. There was a slight departure from routine in that the three sat together in the hall lounge for a symphony program on the radio.

The program ended at ten thirty, when Maud went upstairs to bed. Giving her time to turn the corridor into the west wing, the Millards began to discuss her odd behavior.

Julia thought there was nothing below the surface, but Millard differed.

"She wasn't listening to Beethoven—she was sitting bolt upright in a sort of trance. She might get a brainstorm in the night, slip down the back staircase without our hearing her, and dump herself in the river."

"Oh, nonsense!" Julia was still laughing at him when the history of the Manor House repeated itself.

This time the scream of pain came from the west wing, in a woman's voice. Again the door was locked, Julia ran for the same footstool. Millard stopped her a dozen yards from the door.

"There's no need for us both to go through this. You stay here and keep cool—I'm bound to want your help in a minute."

He smashed the panel and entered the room. Maud was lying half dressed on the floor. On the dressing table was an open box of Athene Chocolates half empty.

"She's dead." He spoke to Julia from the doorway. "Will you call Dr. Blagrove and tell him I'm on my way to pick him up?"

# Chapter Five

Chief Inspector Curwen took over from the local police on the following morning, a Friday. The Millards courteously offered him the house as a headquarters, limiting themselves to two rooms upstairs and taking their meals at restaurants. The inquest, held on Monday, was adjourned after medical evidence that Maud Dacey had died of strychnine poisoning, taken in a chocolate or chocolates at approximately 10:40, Thursday night.

In the meantime, though the facts were few, the publicity was getting into its stride. The Manor House had made the grade as a House of Doom. In 1793, it appeared, the then lord of the manor had been killed by burglars on his own doorstep. The death of Arthur Dacey was recalled, with photographs. They missed the pet cemetery. But this time the 'Tragic story' of Julia was re-told, with photographs of Doris Trallen and the boathouse in which she had died, seven years previously.

Curwen had taken the dining room for himself. When Julia came in, he thought she looked too shattered to talk. He was wrong.

"You've read in the papers about how I accidentally killed a junior girl when I was at school?" she asked as he sat opposite her at the table.

"Of course, we can't prevent 'em printing that kind of thing—"

"Did you know that the child's mother was Mrs. Dacey?—that my father married her six weeks after the accident?"

It was the first time in many years that Curwen had been startled by a witness. His whole approach to the case was threatened.

"It wasn't in the papers," he muttered. "It seems a strange sort of marriage—but has it any bearing on her death?"

"Last Thursday would have been her daughter's twenty-first birthday. Things may have been preying on her mind. She was certainly in a very queer state at dinner that night. But I admit I never thought she would kill herself."

Kill herself! So that was to be the Millards' line! Curwen wanted details—which Julia gave, emphasizing that it was the first time Maud had alluded to the accident.

"Mightn't it have slipped out unintentionally?" suggested Curwen.

"No. She was definitely rubbing it in. It was as if she hated me."

Curwen was trying desperately to piece it together.

"For instance," continued Julia, "I remarked on a brooch she was wearing. She told me that it had belonged to her Doris—and that Doris would have been wearing it that night—if she had lived!"

Curwen was still sceptical.

"Look at it this way, Mrs. Millard. On previous occasions when she was wearing the brooch—"

"She had never worn it before. It was a child's—or a very young girl's—brooch. A showy design of two butterflies, outlined in diamond points and colored stones, probably turquoise. It looked ridiculous on her, and she must have known it. I think she was wearing it *at* me!"

"She might have had some feeling against you on account of the accident—however unjust. Did she ever express it before last night?"

"Never once! We hadn't much in common except our interest in this house. Perhaps that is why we always got on well together. I only hope I was as considerate as she was. I feel mean, telling you about her behavior on Thursday night, but I think it proves she was not her normal self."

But it didn't prove that she contemplated suicide, thought Curwen.

"We shall not know whether Mrs. Dacey killed herself," he asserted, "until we've found where that strychnine came from."

"You know already, Inspector. Obviously, it was she who took the missing five hundred grains from the laboratory."

"Have you any kind of proof?"

"When I have no proof, I fall back on common sense. She could not have got that strychnine except from the laboratory." She was slurring her words as if she were struggling with a sudden sleepiness. *"Heart failure!"* she exclaimed, wide-awake. "The vet told my husband our dog had died of heart failure—which has to be caused by something. Inspector, is it possible that the vet just said heart failure when he knew it was really strychnine?"

"I don't see why a vet should lie about it," hedged Curwen. "It's hardly my business. You'd better ask your husband."

Julia nodded and apologized.

"I see what's in your mind," added Curwen. "Maybe she had a morbid streak. I noticed that pet cemetery in the garden. Someone told me that all her pets had been—sort of murdered—that the parrot had been suffocated."

"Whatever next!" exclaimed Julia. "The parrot died of old age. The others—well, they just died—probably through overfeeding. If anything horrible had been done, I would remember."

Funny she should deny it, he thought—it would have helped her tale. Curwen felt that he was losing his grip on his witness. Her revelation concerning Doris Trallen's mother had distorted the whole grouping of facts. He would work back to Mrs. Millard through her husband.

But her husband distorted the grouping still further. Curwen's opening was based on the knowledge that the opinions of suspected persons are often more revealing than the facts in their possession.

"Mrs. Millard seems to think that deceased killed herself?"

"That's one way of putting it."

"Then put it the right way for me, Mr. Millard."

"She tried to poison my wife, muddled the chocolates, and killed herself by accident. She managed better when she poisoned her husband." Millard hurried on, "It can't matter to you what I think. You want facts. With my wife's help, I've spent the weekend making a log." He handed over a sheaf of typewritten sheets. "All my acts and movements and ditto of the other two as known to me. All correct to a minute or so. Footnotes give any explanations my wife and I thought necessary."

Curwen expressed approval, studied the log for a few minutes,

"Thursday evening. 6:15 gave Maud chocolates," he read aloud. "Later she opens the box and, still further on, puts it on the sideboard." Curwen paused. "I may as well tell you now that the local police found a box of Athene Chocolates on that sideboard, keeping step with your log. There were just two chocolates missing. I had the rest analyzed. Five chocolates, all up at one end, had been impregnated with strychnine. Can you tell us anything about that, Mr. Millard?"

"Only this—the box cannot have been the one I gave her at six fifteen. She couldn't have dolled herself up, doped the chocolates, and refixed the cellophane, all by 7 o'clock. She must have switched the boxes. Try that wastebasket—she threw the cellophane in there."

"You may be right. The cellophane *had* been cut and gummed together again. A box of the same chocolates—rubber-stamped on the cellophane from the Korner House—was found, intact, in her bedroom. All this, as you say, points to the boxes having been switched. But it doesn't tell us *who* switched the boxes and poisoned the chocolates!"

Millard thought it over. Curwen did not disturb him.

"She must have reasoned like this, Inspector," he said. "Julia was to swallow one of the doped chocolates and die in this room. Maud would say I had given her the chocolates and so I would be convicted. It would not have come off, of course, but she knew nothing at all about police methods. We shall never know what she actually did with those chocolates, so we can forget them."

Forget them! To Curwen it seemed an incredibly childish suggestion. Millard was actually going on to talk of something else.

"So I tell my chief," interrupted Curwen, "that we think deceased poisoned herself by accident—but we can't find out how!"

"I don't think I deserved that!" Millard was offended. "If you will pay me the compliment of studying my log—which is checkable throughout—you will find that any one of the three of us could have performed all the monkey tricks of switching boxes and cellophane."

This time it was Millard who waited—still and silent until Curwen looked up from the log.

"You see for yourself, Inspector. The chocolates won't help until you've found out who pinched the five hundred grains of strychnine from the lab."

"We aren't allowed to use magic!"

"You would have been allowed to look for that strychnine in Maud Dacey's deed-box, lodged with a Safe Deposit company. It might have helped you when her husband was killed. I don't say it would have—I say it might have."

"We checked on all the Deposit companies. She had no deed-box on deposit at that time."

"That's where you're wrong, Inspector! *She had!*" To correct a Yard inspector on a statement of fact is no mean achievement and Millard was making the most of it. "She deposited a deed-box before she married Dacey. With Empire Securities, Ltd. The account was in her former name of Trallen. Perhaps that is why you missed it?"

That was a knock for Curwen.

"Why didn't you tell me at the time?"

"Because I'd never heard of that deed-box until about a month ago. She asked me to bring it home for her. I did so."

Curwen went into the hall to telephone.

"I've sent one of our men to check your story with the Deposit company. I expect his report within an hour." Curwen resumed his seat. "You're putting up an idea, but it's a tough one. I can't see that old fuddy-duddy as the Maniac Killer."

"Maniac nothing! She had a sort of hangfire hate for the Daceys. For Mr. Dacey because he married her only out of compassion. She would have killed Julia in this room if I hadn't happened to pass the box and turn it around. Plan Number Two was to leave the box on the sideboard. Julia often accepted her chocolates, but I never did. And she believed that all she had to tell you was that the box was the same one I had given her, and everything would be lovely."

"And did she hate your little dog, too?"

"It's a safe bet—*now*—that she poisoned Chiang. If only because my wife was fond of him. Last night at dinner she worked the hate up to a sort of cold hysteria. She mentioned the accident—which she had never done before. And part of the general build-up was chatter about what the poor kid would be doing at that moment, if Julia hadn't killed her—pretty nearly in those words. She was nerving herself for the poison act. Blind chance and her own clumsiness gave her what she deserved."

Highlight on hate, again, thought Curwen. Both husband and wife were trying to put over a Maud Dacey who was more or less off her head. All very tenuous. Get back to the facts.

Curwen started the routine questioning. The records give 43 questions about the chocolates, without useful result. At the end of an hour he was called to the telephone to hear the Yard's report.

"The company confirms your statement," he announced, beaming. "You've got something there!"

"But very little," replied Millard, gloomily. "Backing for a theory, but no direct evidence. Even Maud would not have been such a fool as to put that phial of strychnine back in the deed-box, knowing that I knew about her using the other name.

"As it is," he went on, "suspicion hangs over me and my wife. It's a million times worse for Julia. Those beastly papers dragging up the old accident—with an oily hint that it might not have been an accident, meaning she's a female Jekyll and Hyde. That sort of thing sticks to a person for life."

"Take it easy," laughed Curwen. "*We* haven't finished yet!"

"You *have* finished!" The words came in an audible whisper. "You've got all the evidence that's gettable. As you did when Arthur Dacey was killed. From your angle, it's the same murder over again. Everybody shoveling information at you—but none of it worth anything without that phial. Why, it must be small enough to be hidden under a single leaf in the garden—or in Hyde Park, for that matter!"

"Just so," agreed Curwen politely. "But we'll begin by looking in that deed-box—as soon as we've found it."

"*What!*" Millard sprang from his chair. "Wasn't it in her room?

Didn't you find it when you searched the house on Friday? Did you search outside the house?"

"We've not been searching for a deed-box, but we'll start right away—we know she didn't return it to Deposit. There was a key on her dressing table we couldn't find a lock for."

"My God, Inspector, I'm trying to take it in! If she has hidden that deed-box, there can be no other reason than—the phial of strychnine! She hid it there once, and she was much too one-track to think of hiding the tiny bottle without also hiding the big tin box. She's probably put it in the cloakroom at the railway station. No, she might have been seen carrying it. She's buried it in the garden—that's it! The pets' graveyard was her special spot. Let's see if the earth has been turned—"

"What about leaving the details to us?" suggested Curwen, with some emphasis. "Thank you for your cooperation, Mr. Millard."

Unaided by Millard, Curwen's men found Maud Dacey's deed-box, within twenty minutes, but not in the pets' cemetery. They began in the garage, climbed by iron rungs to the disused upper part that had once been the groom's quarters before the stables had been converted. The deed-box was under crumbling floorboards, which had been clumsily replaced. On top of the deed-box was a coil of thick cord. The iron rungs were broad and could easily have been negotiated by a middle-aged woman provided she were unencumbered by a skirt. The box could have been hauled up afterwards by the cord.

# Chapter Six

The Millards were unaware that a search had been begun. On leaving Curwen, Millard had rushed upstairs like a schoolboy bursting with news. Indeed, Julia saw him as a schoolboy, excited about a missing deed-box. A clue, no doubt, to something or other. For her, now, there could be only one clue.

"You're barely listening, Julie. What's on your mind?"

"Chiang!" she answered, and instantly the schoolboy in him looked ashamed. "Did he die of strychnine poisoning, Will? Did you know it at the time? Was that why you wouldn't let me go into the sitting room and see him?"

"Oh, damn Curwen!" groaned Millard. "Yes—that is, I could see that he had died violently."

Chiang had died of strychnine! She had dreamed, long before the dog had come into their home, that she had stolen strychnine from the laboratory and hidden it—in order to kill.

"I am sorry I lied to you, Julia. But I believed I had to."

He believed he had to! Her fear of herself was multiplied—the dormant fear that had been fanned by the innuendoes in the newspaper, circling round the old river accident.

"It doesn't matter about the lie part of it. I told you the dreams had stopped after we married. They hadn't."

"I know. You talked in your sleep sometimes. I wanted to help you."

What else about herself had she kept from him?

"I dreamed that I killed Chiang. How do you know I didn't?"

"Darling, that's a very silly question!"

"How do you know I didn't kill father? And Maud? Or do you know that I *did?*"

The schoolboy likeness had now completely vanished. She saw an anxious man—driven into a corner and afraid.

"All right! I'll take it seriously. I can no more prove your innocence than can the police. I just know you are innocent because you are my wife. Recurrent nightmares are common. But a man could not have a schizophrenic wife and not be aware of it."

He was stating his faith in her, but faith had become meaningless.

"Will! Don't you see what you're proving?" She would not let him out of the corner into which she had forced him. "If you knew I had not killed Chiang, you must have believed that Maud did! Let me finish. That means you must have had at least a suspicion that she killed father. Why did you let us come and live with such a woman? She might have killed me, or you, or both of us."

"As a matter of fact, that's what she tried to do. Only—"

"But why did you let us come here? It was an incredible thing to do. But it suddenly becomes a reasonable thing to do if you—*if you* killed Chiang and—"

She broke off. He no longer looked anxious. His face seemed to radiate a vast relief.

"Now, that's a perfectly sensible thing to say!" It was almost as if the suggestion had pleased him. "As Curwen amiably pointed out, I *could* have killed poor little Chiang by forcing the stuff down his throat while you were upstairs. There were money motives for murdering your father—Maud, too, for that matter. In both cases, *you* get more money, but you share it with me, so I benefit. It's one of the three lines the police have been working up. Your guilt, my guilt, Maud's guilt—with the tail-piece that she killed herself by accident."

"But you *didn't*, Will?"

"Never mind! We shall have a hell of a strain waiting for them to find that deed-box. You must keep your head. If you get chattering to Curwen about those dreams, heaven knows what might happen! You don't really feel you have done all this awful killing. You've argued yourself into believing that you *might* have. They're rotten arguments. The arguments pointing to me are ever so much stronger. So let's cut out all arguments and trust the police. Don't tell them one single thing you don't have to tell them. And now I'm going to make some tea. I think that electric kettle is under your bed.

Before the tea was ready, a Yard man knocked at the door.

"Inspector wants you both to come down, please."

The deed-box was on the table in the dining room. One of Curwen's men was dusting it, making a little cloud of white powder; another was adjusting a camera.

"We found this box on the upper floor of your garage," announced Curwen and added, with a grin: "With your permission, we propose to open it in your presence."

With the key from Maud's dressing table he unlocked the box. He raised the lid, glanced inside, and immediately lowered it. He took, from his own bag, a pair of forceps and a flat tin box about a foot square. With the former he lifted from the deed-box a small metal syringe.

"This was used for inserting the poison into the chocolates. It hasn't been wiped." He was speaking to the Millards. "Has either of you seen this before?"

"I don't remember seeing it," said Julia.

"Then you should say you have not seen it before," corrected Millard. "Nor have I, Inspector."

"The next object," said Curwen, forceps in hand, "is a phial. Maybe it's what we've all been looking for." He placed it on the table. "But we don't know yet." He opened his own flat tin box, which contained test tubes and a large number of tiny bottles. "I don't often have to do this job—and chemistry isn't my strong suit—so perhaps you'll be kind enough to check what I'm doing, Mrs. Millard."

"Let me hold the tube," offered Julia. "You put the substance in first, then add the reagent . . . Yes, that's strychnine."

"It's our lucky day, Julia!" cried Millard. "Perhaps Inspector Curwen will excuse you now?"

"I'd be obliged if Mrs. Millard would wait," objected Curwen. "At the moment, this box—for all we know in point of evidence—might be yours, or Mrs. Millard's. We'll have to identify it by the contents."

He took out the framed photographs of the child.

"Mrs. Millard?"

"I've never seen the photos before." Her voice was unsteady. "This child might be Doris Trallen. But I cannot say positively."

"I don't think you'll be able to get an identification from us," put in Millard. "That box was locked away before any of us knew Mrs. Dacey."

"We'll have to run through it, all the same," muttered Curwen. He took out a small jeweler's case and pressed the catch.

"What about this?"

In the case was a brooch—a showy design of two butterflies in diamond points and turquoise.

"Oh, yes!" cried Julia. "That's the brooch she was wearing at dinner—the one I told you about, Inspector. You agree, Will?"

"Could be, but I can't swear to it."

"It will be evidence of identification if you both agree," said Curwen. "Let's see, now." He produced the log which Millard had written. "It's in here, somewhere. Here! '7:05. Dinner. Incidents of dinner: Mrs. D., gaudy, unsuitable dress; brooch (child's), twin butterflies, diamonds, turquoise.' That's what you wrote, Mr. Millard." He displayed the brooch. "It seems to me a fairly accurate description?"

"Good enough!" agreed Millard.

Curwen continued to read from the log. "'After dinner: Beethoven symphony; Mrs. D. inattentive and restless; 10:30, Mrs. D. goes to bed. Mrs. M. and self discuss her strange behavior. 10:40, scream from direction of Mrs. D.'s room.' Hm! At ten thirty she goes up to bed. She takes off the brooch, puts it in this jeweler's case and locks it in the deed-box. Then she removes the gaudy dress—she was found in underthings. How long would all that take her, Mrs. Millard?"

"She couldn't have whipped that dress off," answered Julia, with thought. "With one thing and another, I don't see how she could have done it all in less than five or six minutes."

"Brings us pretty close to ten forty, doesn't it? Leaves her only four or five minutes for the whole job of getting up those rungs—in an underskirt—and getting back to her room to eat the chocolate."

He looked at both of them.

"If Mrs. Dacey hid that deed-box, *she must have done it after she was dead*. You are both under arrest."

"No, we're not, Inspector!" snapped Millard. "Just go on reading. Try the ten forty-five entry."

"'Ten forty-five,'" quoted Curwen. "'Asked Mrs. M. to 'phone Dr. Blagrove that I would pick him up in my car.' What of it?"

"How can you ask!" Millard was elaborately patient. "If that deed-box was taken from that bedroom *after* Mrs. Dacey's death, it must have been taken while my wife was telephoning."

That gave Curwen what he wanted—for already he was sure there was only one guilty person.

"Your wife would have had time enough to hide that deed-box while you were fetching the doctor. Or you yourself could have taken it with you when you went to the garage for the car. Have it your own way, Mr. Millard. We're not required to prove which of you did what. You are jointly charged."

"Will!" cried Julia. "I can't bear this. Is he proving—?"

"Don't interrupt, dear! The inspector is talking to me."

Curwen made no protest as Millard led his wife to the door, kissed her, then shut her out of the room.

"Thanks, Curwen," he said, then nerved himself for the plunge. Julia's instant identification of the brooch had made any defence hopeless.

"While she was telephoning, I took the deed-box down the backstairs and put it under the boards, which I'd fixed beforehand. I killed Arthur Dacey and Maud—and I killed the Peke to lay a trail against Maud. I'm not even warning my wife not to talk to you without a lawyer—the more she talks the better you'll know she had nothing to do with it from start to finish."

Which still leaves some doubt whether Millard could be typed as The Matrimonial Adventurer.

# *A Toy for Jiffy*

# Chapter One

In most civilized countries the procedure in the criminal courts permits every circumstance in the prisoner's favor to be brought out and properly considered. In England—though it is painful to admit it—this does not apply to trial for murder. British law acknowledges two points of favor only—reasonable doubt whether the accused did in fact commit the murder, and, alternatively, proof that he was so mentally deranged at the time that "he did not know that what he was doing was wrong."

Of course, Douglas Baines knew that it was wrong to seize a girl by the throat and try to shake the truth out of her. He did not deny that he had taken twenty pounds from her purse. So the judge colored his address to the jury with a great deal of moral indignation.

But that was because the judge did not know how and why Baines had been caught—five years after the crime had been committed.

Baines was the son of a prosperous architect, practising in York. His mother had run away—eloped—when he was two. But his father had filled the double role so successfully that the boy had been barely conscious of his loss. In 1944, he was eighteen and was therefore swept into the army while on his way to a university to seek a degree in engineering. He had no aptitude for soldiering; but in France he did well enough to be given a Field promotion from the ranks. He was pleased because his father was so pleased.

After the fighting was over, he was sent to London on escort duty, without leave. His job done, he wrongfully took the next train to York—he had not seen his father for more than a year.

After the first glad minutes of reunion, he frankly explained that he was awarding himself a few days' leave. His father's geniality vanished and with it the affection of nineteen years. He ordered the boy to return to his unit at once—or he would himself report to the authorities. The shock was profound. Hating the world and himself, Douglas Baines collected his civilian clothing, emptied his bank account of some fifty pounds, deserted the army and his home at the same time, and came to London.

A deserter—without the identity card and the ration book which were then in force—was in much the same position as an escaped convict, except that there was no publicity and he was not actively hunted. Meals could be bought in restaurants. But it was impossible to obtain lawful employment.

When he was halfway through the fifty pounds, he met Daisy Harker, a waitress in a cheap "caff." She guessed what he was doing. She stimulated his waning courage, gave him practical advice on how to scratch a living, and fell in love with him—as much as Daisy Harker could fall in love with any man. Daisy was spirited, more than a little motherly, and passably good-looking.

He joined forces with her, adopting her surname, and drifted into the life of a "spiv." He was not exactly a crook, though few of his activities would bear the full light of day. It was a life of street-corner deals, of shady little commissions, of sudden repairs to a car, with no questions asked. He endured it contentedly enough until Daisy bore him a son. Thereafter, his single purpose was to wriggle himself into a legitimate business.

It so happens that the whole of his life for the next four years is compressed and, as it were, photographed in the last half hour of Daisy's life.

It was early evening of a foggy day in November. He clattered down the stairs to the basement flat, in a slum area near Euston Station. The clattering alone was significant, for the years of spivving had given him a catlike walk. He was carrying a neatly wrapped parcel bearing the imprint of a toy shop. He had the air of a man who has won a sweepstake and is warning himself to keep his head.

The house—a tumbledown Victorian survival—was let by the

floor. It was damp and drafty, but at least it provided space. The kitchen-living room was like two rooms in one. In the kitchen half was the stove, overhung with a wash line on which underclothes were drying, and an oilcloth-covered table at which were three chairs, the third being a young child's high-chair. The sitting room part contained two aged armchairs and a settee in faded plush.

He called to Daisy, received no answer, and promptly forgot her. He sat at the table and with slow enjoyment unwrapped the parcel. From the carton he took a tumbler doll, a garish clown made of tin: it was so weighted that when it was pushed over from any angle, it would noisily wobble back to a standing position. Baines pushed it and giggled happily as it wobbled back.

Daisy came in from the bedroom. She had reached home only a few minutes before himself. She was still wearing a neat outdoor skirt and her best blouse, and carried her purse bag in the crook of her arm. She looked from the toy to the paper in which it had been wrapped.

"Did you *buy* that thing?"

"Paid cash over the counter—and liked it! Bert paid up this morning and a good time will be had by all." He glanced over his shoulder, to make sure the bedroom door was shut—in case the boy should be awake. "Jiffy didn't know it was his birthday last Thursday, unless you told him, so his birthday is tomorrow, see? Take a look at this, will you!" He poked the toy. "You can't help laughing!"

"Kids don't play with toys like that."

"Jiffy will!" He pushed the toy out of reach. "Listen, Daise, I've got a bit of good news."

"You always have got a bit of good news."

"Hark at her!" A laugh rippled up from deep down. "This is different, Daisy. This is a real opening at last!"

"I'm sure it is." She was bitter. "You met a man in a pub who has a gem of an idea and enough dough to get it started. And it's legitimate business—or next door to. And in a month you'll have an office of your own and we'll get a decent place to live in. You'll go on having that bit o' good news all your life."

"Say it all!" His eyes were smiling. "Only this time, duckie, you'll be wrong. This man is in a good way of business."

"Did he happen to ask what you've been doing these last few years? . . . Whatcher tell him?"

"I told him I deserted from the army and I'm still on the run." He saw that he had shaken her, and pressed on, "Do you know what he said Daise? He said, 'I got browned off on my last leave, too. But I was luckier than you,' he says. 'My missis—she was the girlfriend then—she nagged me into going back to duty. And now I've got a repair garage and I'm getting another and I need a manager.' Meaning *me!*"

Daisy was silenced but not convinced. His tales were never downright lies, though nothing ever came of them.

"Think of it, Daisy! It means an end of all this. It means I'll be able to look Jiffy in the face when he's old enough to ask questions." She remained unimpressed. "We're going to celebrate. There's a half bottle of mother's ruin in my coat. And put some grub up, I'm starving."

He got up, moved towards the bedroom door.

"What're you going in there for?" she asked.

"It's all right—I won't wake him."

"Jiffy isn't in his cot," she said sullenly.

"Cor! You oughtn't to've left him at Ma Dawson's as late as this." A second later his good temper returned. "I'll go and fetch him while you get the grub."

"Stay where you are, Douglas!" The tone of her voice stopped him short. "Jiffy's gone. I've fixed it for him to be adopted. I took him along to his new mum and dad this afternoon."

"Say that again!" He was trying to force time backwards to the moment before she had said it.

"I made up my mind months ago. A gentleman friend who's a lawyer told me I have a perfect right and you can't do anything. And he's seen to the law part of it for me. Better get used to it, Doug. You'll never see that kid again."

He was standing where he had stopped on his way to fetch Jiffy. He was not even looking at her.

"They're decent people, if you want to know—real gentry, with money of their own. They'll give him a proper chance.... First and last he's my child, don't forget it.... I'll own up you'd have done your best for him, but your best wouldn't have been any good. Done him harm, more like ... If I've never been a good mother to him before, I've been one today."

Slowly the essential question framed itself.

"How much did they give you?"

"Twenty quid, though I don't see what that's got to do with it, I suppose you want your cut. You do need a couple o' new shirts."

"We're going to pay it back. Tonight. Before they have time to get fond of Jiffy."

She stormed at him, arguing that the adopting parents would send for the police if he made a scene and the police would ask unanswerable questions. Baines was thinking of something else.

"Jiffy will be frightened in a strange place. Betcher he's howling for me this very minute. I'm going to get him."

That loosed in her the frustration of years and the submerged hatred.

"You, slopping over that kid!" she shrilled. "Look him in the face when he's old enough and—kiss-me-foot! Will you tell him you let his mother keep you when you daren't go to the hospital because of being a deserter? And you pretending to believe I got all that cash-on-the-nail as a waitress in a caff! You'd got eyes, same as other men. You could see where that money came from."

"It doesn't matter what I've been. Everything's different now." His own words came as a revelation to him. Life was beckoning to him and Jiffy. "Put your hat and coat on and take me along to those people—and I'll marry you as soon as you like. It'd be safe now."

"*You'll marry me!* Thank you kindly, Mister Whatever-your-name-is—I don't know because you've never told me. And you can drink that half bottle o' gin by yourself because I'm walking out on you tonight!"

"Okay! I'll settle about Jiffy myself. You're out of it and no one will blame you. Give me the address and mind it's the right one."

"So's you can make a nasty smell round his new life before it's even begun! Not me!"

As she passed his chair he caught her wrist and bent it.

"What's the address?"

When she refused, he gripped her round the neck and slowly applied pressure.

"You'll break my neck, you fool!"

She was not frightened enough—not yet. But as the pressure increased, she screamed. The scream was cut off and he felt a click that might have come from her bones. Her weight sagged onto his hands, and he lowered her gently to the floor.

"Daisy ... Daisy, snap out of it.... I'll get you a drink." He knew it would be absurd to get her a drink. But, again, he had to reach back—to the moment before he had killed her. He even took the bottle from his raincoat, but was jerked back to reality by the sound of footsteps—shuffling footsteps which he recognized—coming down to the basement.

The new life had not yet begun—the technique of the old still had its uses. He flung his raincoat over the child's high-chair and moved the chair so that a man standing in the doorway would have no line of vision to the corpse. Then he shouted as if he were still brawling with a living woman.

"You got what was coming to you! And now go and wash your face." Then he opened the door to the elderly tenant of the floor above.

"Why, it's you, Mr. Hendricks! Fact is, I lost my temper and dotted her one. She's washing herself up. P'raps you'd like to see her, so's you can tell Mrs. Hendricks it's all right? ... Hi, Dais-*ee*! Here's Mr. Hendricks wants to know what it's all about. Come in, Mr. Hendricks, she won't be a minute."

But Mr. Hendricks, as could be anticipated, declined the invitation and shuffled back up the stairs.

Baines was now fully alert. He found the same shabby old suitcase with which he had left his father's house, and began to pack. As he was about to leave he caught sight of Daisy's purse on the floor.

He picked it up, sat at the table, and opened it. From the litter inside he drew a wad of currency notes.

Twenty pounds.

He was stuffing the notes in his pocket when his elbow knocked against the tumbler doll and set it wobbling. It clattered on the table and inside his head. His sense of time slipped—it was as if the clatter would never stop. He tried to put out his hand to stop it.

The fantasy passed. That twenty pounds had been the price paid for Jiffy. He sprang up and went to the stove. In the act of thrusting the notes inside, he pulled up.

"I must show *some* sense. All right! I'll show some sense." The notes went into his pocket.

Turning round, he faced the tumbler doll. He decided to destroy it—and an instant later was horrified at his own decision. He put it back in its carton, then made room for it in the suitcase by throwing out a pair of gum boots.

# Chapter Two

On the following day the total silence in the basement alarmed Mrs. Hendricks, who told the rent collector, who in turn informed the police. They traced the recent movements of "Douglas Harker," including the purchase of the gin—which he had left behind—and the tumbler doll, traced through the wrapping paper. The time of the purchase suggested that he did not know his child had already gone to the foster parents—which might have been the cause of the quarrel. The absence of the toy from the basement suggested that a murderer on the run had encumbered himself with a bulky, mass-produced toy, worth only a few shillings and difficult to resell. Possible but unlikely—and certainly not helpful!

The dragnet went out for Douglas Harker, with police description, and yielded nothing—because Harker, the streetcorner commission agent, had, in effect, ceased to exist.

The history of Douglas Baines for the next five years is a commonplace one of steady if unspectacular success. The war restrictions were now gone and a man could move as freely and anonymously as he liked. His own name, being a fairly common one, no longer held danger.

True, the first three months at the garage had taxed his abilities. Encouraged by the faith of his employer, however, he survived and soon took the initiative. The repair service grew and added a sales agency, the trade boom acting as Baines's fairy godmother. He was able to rent a serviced flat in a respectable district.

In appearance he was a tall, well groomed businessman, looking a little older than his thirty years. His personality reverted to type. His outlook, his tastes, and his habits became those which one would have expected from his early upbringing. The years of spivving seemed to have left no traces—with one exception.

We again receive a telling picture of Baines by watching his behavior with a woman—in this case, Joan Mencefield. She was a first-grade secretary who lived in a flat of her own in Chelsea. The attraction had been mutual—perhaps strengthened by the girl's perception that there was a shadow in the man's background.

They were having tea in his flat when he asked her to marry him.

"Yes, of course I will!" He had been rather solemn and hesitant about it. "In June, if you like," she said. "It will have to be a quiet one—Mother is hard up. You bring two friends and I'll bring two—that sort of wedding. You don't mind, do you? Why, you're not listening!"

"I've been trying to ask you for months. But I felt I had to tell you something about myself, first. I kept putting it off."

"Then don't tell me—I'll tell you instead." She invited his kiss. "My dear, dear man! Your secret writes itself all over your face every time your car is stopped at a crossing by—young school children. Little boys, about seven to nine years old."

"I'd no idea I was giving myself away like that!" He was pleased, because now they could share his secret. "I'm not always thinking about him, only sometimes!"

"I suppose his mother is part of the problem?" she asked.

"Oh, no!" It was as if she had asked a pointless question. "She's dead and out of it."

He had not forgotten that he had killed her. He blamed himself—much as a car driver who had killed another in a road smash might acknowledge to himself a measure of blame. The sense of personal peril had long vanished.

"I want to be told only one thing, Douglas—is the boy alive?"

That shattered his contentment.

"I don't know!" It sounded worse when he said it aloud. "Why shouldn't he be alive and happy? With people who are always kind to him? It's just as likely to be that way as—the other."

He suspected that he was telling her about it in the wrong way. He warned himself to speak calmly and clearly.

"He was adopted. His mother fixed it behind my back. When I came home one evening he was gone. Gone for good! I never saw him again. But that's all over—it doesn't affect me now."

"Only sometimes?"

Her sympathy was weakening his grip on himself.

"Five years ago, it was. He was just three. I'd bought him a toy. And when I got home, he wasn't there. I couldn't give him his birthday present. See what I mean? I never saw him play with it."

She could not fail to notice the change in him and censured herself for stirring memories that still disturbed him. Before she could turn the conversation, he added:

"Matter of fact, I have the toy still. Like to see it, Joan?"

"Only if you're quite sure you want to show it to me."

Before she had answered he was unlocking a drawer in the writing table. The carton was crinkled now, but the colors of the clown were as garish as ever. He drew a chair for himself, sat at the table, and gazed at the doll.

Joan watched him with deep concern. She guessed that he had slipped into a world of his own. He was smiling now, but not at her. When he broke into speech she observed the change in his voice.

"Take a look at this, will you! You can't help laughing." He thrust with a finger at the clown. "O-ver he goes! ... Up again and roundabout. Now it's your turn, Jiffy. Knock him over, boy! That's the way."

He was laughing in counterpoint with the clatter of the toy—the timed, mechanical laughter of a self-induced trance in which he was playing with his child.

Without warning he looked up at her.

"That's torn it!" he said quietly. "I didn't know I was as far gone as that, or I would not have asked you to marry me. We'll call it off, Joan."

"You thought I wanted you to say that—but I don't!" She thrust her arm through his and held him close to her. There was a long silence.

"Do you often play with it?"

"No. I can't remember," he faltered. She waited and he added: "Yes. Quite often."

"Let me keep it for you." She sensed his opposition and hurried on. "You know it's bad for you. If you will trust me with it, I'll lock it away. And I promise I'll give it back at once, whenever you ask, day or night."

"Day or night," he echoed. "How could you keep such a promise? You might not be at home. You're going to your mother's next weekend, and you'll not be back until Monday morning."

That told her that it must be now or never.

"Here is the key to my flat—and here's the key of the left-hand drawer of my dressing table. You can keep them—I have duplicates." Before he could speak, she added: "I think it's our only chance, Douglas—if we are ever to have a child of our own."

Her meaning was sufficiently clear. He wanted her very much and would not risk losing her for the sake of a melancholic dream. He put the toy in its carton and handed it to her.

The next time he saw her—which was also the last time—was on the following Monday morning.

# Chapter Three

He was finishing breakfast when he heard her knock. He got up slowly, puzzled, and opened the door.

She stepped quickly over the threshold, took the latch from his hand, and shut the outer door.

"Douglas! I've let you down, though it wasn't my fault. The toy!"

She had feared some kind of breakdown but he gave no sign of distress.

"I was having breakfast," he said. "There's some tea left. Come along."

She assumed he had not understood. She signed to him not to pour out tea and made a new beginning.

"Bad news! While I was away, sneak-thief burglars got into the flat. They took my nice rug, most of my clothes, all my sheets and blankets, emptied all the drawers on the floor, and left all the windows open so that the rain—"

"That's tough luck!" he broke in. "But you are insured, and there need be no loss in the end. I've lots of blankets and that sort of thing which I can lend you."

"Stop, please! I am trying to break it gently. The toy you entrusted to me for safe-keeping is gone."

"No, it isn't." He was standing by the window, looking out. "I have it."

"Do you mean you took it from the flat before the burglary?"

"Yes. There was no sign of a burglary then."

"Oh, Douglas! I don't know whether to be glad or sorry. Less than a week! I did think you meant to make a real effort."

"I did and I do. I feel very bad about this, Joan. I think it was your going away that did it. The feeling didn't start until Saturday morning, when I thought of you getting on the early train. Then it—well, it sort of grew. It was pretty strong on Saturday evening, but I stuck it out. I fought it on Sunday, but after I'd gone to bed I couldn't hold out any longer. So I dressed and drove over to Chelsea."

She was struck with a sudden happy suspicion.

"I can only half believe you. Are you making it all up to save my feelings? Let me see the toy—please, Douglas." When he unlocked the drawer, showed her the doll, and replaced it, she gave up hope of him.

"You despise me, don't you?" he asked.

"Hardly that." His contrition played on her pity. "It's easy for me to feel superior about it, because I've never had the kind of shock you had. Let's talk about it some other time."

She was about to go when there came a knock on the outer door, and she waited for him to answer it. A moment later she recognized the voice of Detective-Sergeant Jarman, who was investigating the burglary.

"Do you want me, Sergeant?" she asked.

"No, Miss. I didn't know you were here."

"Miss Mencefield and I are engaged to be married," said Baines.

"That should tidy it up," grinned Jarman. "It's about your car, Mr. Baines." He quoted the number. "I have a note that it was parked in Graun Street—that's the side street on the east of the flats—at midnight."

"Correct. But it was there for only a few minutes and I think I can clear myself of the burglary. As you know, Miss Mencefield was away—"

"That's all right, Mr. Baines, now that we know the car was not borrowed for the raid. This gang always uses a private car, which they pick up. They always go for a hundred pounds' worth of domestic stuff, and they do two raids a week—small profits and quick returns, you might say. Sorry to have troubled you, sir."

Thus the district police had an amiable exchange with the

murderer of Daisy Harker, without causing him a tremor. It would have been fantastic to assume that he had been concerned in the burglary. No brilliance of detection could have linked the position of that car, at that time, with the murder—but it was for this sort of thing that the Department of Dead Ends existed.

# Chapter Four

Scotland Yard was not called in. It was a small case, with no outstanding feature. But the fact that the windows had been left open rated five lines in an evening paper. The paragraph was read by Detective-Inspector Rason.

"Builder Smith!" exclaimed Rason, and promptly set out for the local police station. Some two years previously, in a similar burglary in Plymouth, the porter of the flats had been maimed for life, and his assailant was believed to be an ex-builder who had never been caught. Builder Smith was known to be in the habit of opening all the windows while working, though he generally shut them when he had finished.

The local station gave him all its information, which helped him little but kept up his spirits. The constable who had observed the number of Baines's car had observed nothing else, as he had been "proceeding" along the side street. Rason thought the owner of the car might be more helpful.

Rason had the integrity, but few of the other qualities, of a good detective. But the Department of Dead Ends was greater than its servants and required of them not brilliance but enthusiasm—and a long memory. Rason would lurch along a trail of hopes and guesses, and the success—in this case and in others—was due to the logic inherent in the Department itself.

After surveying the site of the flats, with special reference to the side street, he called on Douglas Baines.

Baines, who had half expected the police would turn up again with supplementary questions, was very genial about it.

"I warn you I've already told all I know," he said as he invited Rason into the sitting-room.

"That's all right, Mr. Baines. I'm working on another angle." Rason liked the look of the flat—nothing showy or antique—good modern stuff—the sort of flat he would have himself if he could afford it. He gave a racy sketch of the life and works of Builder Smith.

"Well, I'd like to help you, Mr. Rason, but I don't see how I can, so let's have a little whiskey."

Rason accepted. He gave instances of the activities of Builder Smith which an intelligent man like Mr. Baines might have observed.

"But the burglars turned up after I'd gone—I was back here a little after twelve thirty."

Rason blinked.

"The local police don't know what time it was done."

"Nor do I," said Baines. "But I can tell you quite positively that the flat had not been burgled when I entered it at about five past twelve."

"You were *in* that flat!" Rason hesitated. "I know you won't mind my asking this sort of question, Mr. Baines, but how did you get in? I understand Miss Mencefield was away for the weekend."

"I know. I got in with a latchkey."

Rason was not suspicious of anything—he was merely bewildered.

"If you knew the lady wasn't there—I mean, what was the point of going to the flat at that time of night?"

"It isn't *that* kind of latchkey!" Baines spoke severely. "We're engaged and expect to be married very shortly. We run in and out of each other's flats, to fetch this or leave that. It's fairly common, nowadays."

Rason tried to work it out. Fetch this or leave that. At midnight. When the other person wasn't there. Fairly common?

"It sounds all right, in a way." He drained his glass. "Were you fetching something or leaving something that particular time?"

Baines allowed himself to show irritation.

"Don't think me starchy, old man, but has that anything to do with your—Builder Smith?"

"You'd be surprised, but it has! I'll give you the lowdown." Rason enjoyed expounding police doctrine—which he himself so rarely followed. "We go out on all sorts of cases and ask all sorts of questions of innocent persons. One of the first things that's rubbed into us as recruits is never to pass an answer which we don't understand—no matter what it's about and no matter what kind of person we're talking to."

"I didn't mean to make a mystery of it," said Baines apologetically. "I was going to fetch something. Something very personal, and I hope you won't ask me for details."

"And something mighty urgent that couldn't wait until the lady came home, so you had to go and fetch it at midnight? Something you had to get hold of there and then?"

"True, in a sense. But it's nothing illegal nor indecent—nor even particularly private. It's just something—well, damned ridiculous."

"So when my chief asks me why you went to that flat at midnight I tell him it was for something damned ridiculous?"

Baines's reluctance had nothing to do with the fact that the other man was a detective. The murder of Daisy was not in his present consciousness. Even if it had been, his attitude to the detective would probably have remained the same. It would have been beyond his conception that the tumbler doll could be a clue to the old murder. It had not been left on the scene of the crime. Nor could he guess that the police had ever known he had ever possessed such a thing.

"Fair enough!" Baines felt as if he were about to strip before a hostile crowd. "It's a toy—a child's toy."

Rason did not laugh. He was surprised only that the other had made all that fuss about a toy—if it really was about a toy.

"Now you've cleared that up, have another drink?" invited Baines, pouring it as he spoke.

"Here's luck, Mr. Baines!" Rason set down the glass and added, "Better let me see the toy and then I can cross it off."

Rason meant no more than he said. Nothing could be further from his mind than to connect this respectable man, in his comfortable flat, with the crime committed by a street-corner spiv five years ago. Nor could the toy itself provide a link. It had not been featured in the report. The only mention of it occurred at the end of the inventory, and it had but a couple of lines: *Objects unaccounted for: Tumbler doll bought by Harker circa 5.45; not received by foster parents*—followed by the latter's name and address.

Baines was unlocking the drawer in his writing table. He took out the carton, removed the toy, and placed it on the table.

"There you are. That's the whole mystery."

The appearance of the doll moved Rason to reminiscence only.

"I know those things—my niece had one when she was a nipper." He poked the doll. "Hm! Amusing! Only you'd get tired of it, wouldn't you! What do they call 'em? 'Acrobatic doll'—no, 'Tin Tumbler'?"

"I don't know what they call it." Baines was gazing at the doll. "It's a clever bit of nonsense. A small child would sort of think it's alive and make a pal of it." He began to put it back.

"It's your property and you lent it to Miss Mencefield. So that she could play with it by herself?"

"It isn't quite like that. Anyhow, she will confirm that she was keeping it for me."

Rason had only one more question.

"I take it, then, that you got a strong feeling in the middle of the night that you must have that—that acrobatic doll—to play with?"

"If you like to put it like that," admitted Baines. "I suppose it's a sort of tic in the brain. You'll understand now why I wasn't keen to talk about it."

Baines replaced the toy in the drawer. As the lock clicked Rason exclaimed, "'Tumbler Doll'! That's what they call 'em ... Tumbler Doll," he repeated. "Reminds me of something ... a case in our files. About five years ago, it must've been. Let's see, now—how did the tumbler doll come into it?"

That gave Baines his first suspicion of danger. But suspicion was not enough.

"I've got it! A murder job, it was. Name of Harker. A small-time crook."

It had come too quickly for him—Baines knew he had flinched. But Rason did not observe this, because he had not yet connected Baines with the old ease.

"Harker had a young child—and he seems to have been fond of it. Chaps like that often do turn out to be good fathers, though you'd hardly believe it. Harker must've thought a lot of his because he bought the tot one of those tumbler dolls. When he got home he found his missis had had the kid adopted without telling him. So he broke her neck and hopped it."

Baines relaxed. There was no danger, after all—no more than there had been for every hour of every day for the past five years. His confidence had been strengthened—the police could chat to him about his own crime without the flicker of a suspicion.

Rason was rattling on.

"Funny thing! That tumbler doll wasn't found in the basement, where they lived. Our men never did find it. Vanished. Almost makes one superstitious when you come to think of it."

"I can guess that one," said Baines. "The spiv posted it to the foster parents?"

"No," said Rason. "We checked."

"What sort of people would adopt the child of a spiv?" asked Baines.

"I don't know what they were like—never saw them. We only kept the name and address in case Harker should try to see his child. Which he never has." Rason got up from the armchair which he so deeply approved. "Well, I've taken up a lot of your time, Mr. Baines, and I'll be off."

Rason glanced guiltily at the clock. He had spent half an hour finding out nothing about Builder Smith.

"Have one for the road," suggested Baines.

"No, really, thanks! I'd like to sit here yarning with you, but I've got to make a move."

"Just one more!" Baines poured the whiskey. "You won't do any more detecting tonight, and this is a quick one."

"That's very nice of you. A quick one it is, and I won't sit down again . . . Cheers!"

"That yarn of yours about the spiv's child who was adopted. Five years ago, you said. I think I can put a cap on it. Five years ago a married cousin of mine adopted a boy—took him from surroundings very close to your description. My cousin's name is Gramshaw and he lives at Brighton. I bet that's the name in your files."

Rason gaped at his own face in the wall mirror. What was there in that face which encouraged amateurs to believe they could pull a fast one on him?

He was silent so long that Baines asked, "Well? Am I right?"

"Yes," said Rason.

This time he was watching Baines, and saw the other's jaw drop in sheer astonishment. Rason laughed.

"One of the *other* first things they rub into us as recruits is how to use a trick question and join it up with another." The trick question had given him a new perspective of the man who had to play with a tumbler doll at midnight. "You're better at it than me. 'What sort of people would adopt the child of a spiv?' I fall for it—like the sucker I am—and let you know I know the name and address. But you overdid it with an imaginary 'cousin Gramshaw.' I did *not* answer with another name and address. When I said 'yes,' you nearly had a fit. You *had* to have that address same as you have to have that doll to play with—and for exactly the same reason."

Baines took the second shock steadily.

"And are you going to tell that fantastic story to your chief?"

"Catch me!" smiled Rason. "He'd say it was all guesswork—without a jot of evidence. Won't breathe a word to anybody until we've checked on your fingerprints and shown you to old Hendricks and all the others who lived above your basement . . . Cor, you must be fond of that child! Why the hell did you have to insist on that last whiskey when all I wanted was to go home?"

*Marion, Come Back*

# Chapter One

The murder of Marion Pinnaker ("Mrs. Pin" in the headlines) was a popular mystery, though the Press hated it. Time was an active factor—the mystery grew more mysterious every week merely because the week had passed. After the first fine flare-up, the papers could neither feed it nor kill it.

The mystery had the added charm of simplicity. There was only one popular suspect—her husband. After a preliminary examination, however, the police showed exasperatingly little interest in him. He had the means and the opportunity and it was simple enough to equip him with most of the traditional motives. His peccadilloes could easily be viewed as depravities. On the other hand, his virtues made it easy to see him as the unfortunate victim of slander.

The Pinnakers lived in a detached, six-room house with garden and garage—named "Hillfoot," by grace of a modest slope—in the dormitory suburb of Honshom, which is thirty-two miles out of London. Nearly all the houses are of the same kind and so are the residents—that *is*, they present a united front of respectability, neighborliness, and adequacy of income.

In such a neighborhood people tend to know each other's affairs, as well as each other's movements. No one had seen Marion leave home at a relevant time. Within forty-eight hours there were whispers that she had not left the house at all and would shortly be found under the floorboards.

Tom Pinnaker, armed with a degree in commerce, had entered Bettinson's to begin at the bottom. In the furniture department he learned upholstery; in the catering department he acquired knowledge of wines and cold storage. He was in a straight line for managerial rank when his father died and he took over a small but steady house agency in central London specializing in the renting of small office suites.

The Pinnakers were a little better off than most of their neighbors because, in the second year of their marriage, Marion inherited twenty thousand pounds. She had placed half with her husband for investment. Although this money loomed large in the case there was never anything wrong with Tom Pinnaker's accounts. His losses were due strictly to bungling.

The legacy had come as a surprise—at least, to Tom. It had been a marriage of mutual attraction—which is itself a bit of a mystery because their temperaments were so different. Marion was no glamour girl, to stampede a man's judgment. Among the millions who saw her photograph on television, opinion seemed to be divided—which means that she was attractive to some and not to others. Her face suggested a grave young woman who could be gay, but with the gaiety of a family gathering. A domesticated woman, one would say—remembering that domesticity is highly esteemed by men of many different kinds.

Pinnaker loved his home. He also loved his wife, in his fashion, and was proud of her rigid code of morals: after five years of marriage he would not have changed her for any other kind of woman. Not that he despised all the other kinds. One's character, he told himself, had many facets. There was the facet that had enjoyed fun and games with a business girl in London—doing no harm, he convinced himself, to anybody. And at Honshom there had been—and still was—Freda Culham.

Except for occasional nights in London and sometimes a weekend—attributed to the social demands of clients—his habits were regular: he would never leave home earlier than nine, nor return earlier than six thirty.

Routine was broken on the afternoon of Tuesday, January 5, 1954, when he arrived home a few minutes before three. The official police narrative begins with his entering his house at three. But we can profitably go back one hour—to two o'clock, when Mrs. Harker, the domestic help, entered the sitting room to report that she had finished her work and was going home.

Mrs. Pinnaker, she said, was not dressed—meaning that she was wearing an overall over skirt and sweater, and house shoes. She was sitting at the writing table handling "funny looking papers" (which turned out to be Bearer Bonds) which she was placing one by one in a small attaché case.

Mrs. Harker was conscientiously rude to anyone in a higher income bracket than her own. When she eventually appeared on television she snapped and snarled at the interviewer, expressed her feelings freely without regard to her briefing, and was a huge success. She had a deep regard for Marion.

"You only picked at that grilled sole and I know it was done just as you like it," she grumbled. "To say nothing of the veal cutlets yesterday! And you're thinner than looks healthy. It's not my business, dear, but why don't you see a doctor?"

"There's nothing wrong with me, Mrs. Harker." Marion rarely used first names and never called anybody "dear." "I've been advised to—well, to take a sort of holiday."

"Good advice, too! Take it. I'll manage here all right." She noticed a sealed envelope on the television set. "D'you want that letter posted?"

"No, thanks. It's—"

"Then, if there's nothing else, I'll be off."

"Just a minute, Mrs. Harker." From a drawer in the writing table Marion took out a small jeweler's case, opened it, and displayed a diamond brooch. "On your daughter's wedding day—next Saturday isn't it?—I want you to give her this. That is, if you think she'd like it."

Mrs. Harker protested at the munificence of the gift.

"Don't think about it like that. But if you feel you must, just remind yourself that you've done mnch more for us than you were paid for. And now you must hurry or you'll miss your bus."

That incident could be interpreted as a kind of farewell; but the important point is that the bus touched its stopping point on schedule, at two twelve, and that Mrs. Harker caught it.

A few minutes later Freda Culham turned up. Instead of leaving her car on the street, as would be usual, she drove in. A postman happened to notice the car—satisfactorily identified—standing between the kitchen door and the garage, within five minutes of half-past two.

Freda provided a triangle motive for those who felt that the mystery would be incomplete without it—though there is evidence that Tom Pinnaker had no ambition to make Freda his wife. She was the daughter of a professor and the widow of a test pilot who, between them, had left her enough to live by herself in her own house in Honshom. A lively brunette in her middle twenties, with no occupation.

She records that she came in a friendly spirit to admit that she had fallen in love with Tom Pinnaker, to apologize for causing scandal, and to express the hope that she had not given Marion any pain. She may have dressed it up like that, but it is unlikely. She was untroubled with anything resembling a social conscience. To her, marriage meant little more than a formal announcement that you intended to live with somebody until further notice.

The conversation took place in the hall, both women standing. Freda towered over Marion but otherwise was at a disadvantage. Indeed her friendliness, if any, was wasted on Mrs. Pinnaker.

"I think, Mrs. Culham, you are about to suggest that we should arrange a divorce. I am sorry that I cannot agree. For reasons which you would not appreciate I would in no circumstances whatever divorce my husband."

There were arguments by Freda, unanswered by Marion, but our present concern is that Freda had left the house before Tom Pinnaker arrived at three o'clock.

His account of his movements on entering the house has an unusual crispness. He did not claim a mental "blackout" nor any clouding of memory. He said that he entered the house by the kitchen door, shouted that he had come home. Receiving no answer, he went into the sitting room where his eye was caught by an envelope, propped up on the television set. It was addressed *Tom*, in Marion's handwriting. This made him quite certain that Marion had left him. He put the note, unopened, in his pocket. This was not absent-mindedness. He was positive, he said, that he knew the substance of what his wife had written.

At ten past three he was speaking on the telephone to his bank manager in London. That morning he had asked for the loan of one thousand pounds, promising that his wife would provide the necessary collateral.

"Infernal luck—my wife has been called away to a sick relation. I want you to ring James Roden, manager of the branch here. He's secretary of our tennis club and a personal friend—he will confirm my statement to you that my wife has securities of her own to the value of at least ten thousand pounds. Deposited with him."

At three forty the local bank manager, Roden, rang Hillfoot. He first asked for Marion, and was told about the sick relation.

"Look, Pin. I've just had a call from your branch in London. I'm sorry, but I can't help at all."

"That's all right, Jim. I know you can't talk about clients' affairs. But you did not deny that you hold securities of Marion's?"

"I did deny it—I had to! Marion closed her account here yesterday."

These two conversations on the telephone were much quoted as indicating that Pinnaker must have been telling the truth when he asserted that Marion had left the house before three. But those who preferred The Floorboards Theory suggested that, as soon as he came in, he asked her to provide securities, that when she refused he lost his temper and killed her, probably without intending to, and that the telephone talks were a blind.

When Mrs. Harker brought his breakfast tray on the following morning she ignored his greeting and glared at him.

"Is she coming back today?"

"If you mean Mrs. Pinnaker—no. I expect her to be away for at least a fortnight." He sat down and opened the newspaper. "You might get her room done this morning, then we can lock it up until she comes back."

"And another thing, Mr. Pinnaker! You let the furnace out last night. D'you want me to light it?"

"No, thanks. There's no sense in keeping the house heated night and day—I shall be home very little. I'll use the stoves. You can keep warm in the kitchen, can't you?"

Pinnaker had reached the marmalade stage when Mrs. Harker returned.

"Where has she gone?"

"At the moment, I don't know. She didn't leave word. I expect she'll telephone during the day. What's upsetting you, Mrs. Harker?"

"Her luggage, Mr. Pinnaker! She didn't take any. You can't count that little attaché case that wouldn't hold any clothes. Her suitcases are in the glory-hole under the stairs. *All* her clothes are in her room. She must have gone out on that bitter day in just an overall and jumper. No furs. No coat. Wearing those blue house shoes with soles like paper."

Pinnaker was unable to suggest an explanation.

"I know what might have happened, Mr. Pinnaker—but I won't say I believe it did."

"Let's have it, Mrs. Harker—straight from the shoulder."

"That old Buick you've been trying to sell If somebody brought it back again yesterday afternoon she might have got straight in and driven herself away without thinking what she was doing. And small wonder after all she's been through!"

"No good! I sold the Buick on Monday. That reminds me—I must send a receipt and the log—"

"Never mind that now!" Mrs. Harker nerved herself to ask the crucial question. Her words crept out in a near whisper.

"*What've you done to her?*"

"A great deal that I ought not to have done, Mrs. Harker, and I'm ashamed." He was playing for sympathy and getting it. "Most of it was through thoughtlessness, but that's no excuse. As a result, she has left me. I didn't want anybody to know because I hoped she would return in a week or two. I still hope she will. I didn't want you to know, so I tried to dodge your questions. For that I apologize."

"You haven't done *me* any harm. But you must have upset her extra special and driven the poor girl off her head. People must have turned round and stared at her—going out in an overall in January! She may have caught pneumonia and that's why she hasn't telephoned for her clothes. Or had an accident. Or lost her wits. What about asking the police to ask the hospitals?"

With some reluctance Pinnaker consented, provided Mrs. Harker would come with him.

"I want you to back me up. Tell them everything you know—especially that bit about her not taking any of her clothes. Between us we must convince the police that it's not a case of a wife walking off with a lover. They'll pay more attention to you than to me."

The nearest police station was in the town of Kingbiton, four miles Londonward. Pinnaker gave a brief outline to the superintendent—not mentioning the clothes—then left Mrs. Harker with him and drove on to his office.

Mrs. Harker returned by bus and put in a couple of hours work at Hillfoot. In that time she thoroughly cleaned and tidied Marion's bedroom. Before she left at two o'clock she had answered one caller in person and four inquiries by telephone. In sum, she told the neighborhood that she did not know where Mrs. Pinnaker had gone, how long she would be away, nor when she had left. These statements met and clashed with the bank manager's information about a sick relation.

In the early evening there were more inquiries, some containing a trap, in which Pinnaker was invariably caught.

Kingbiton had forwarded a report to Missing Persons, Scotland Yard. By midday on Thursday they had picked up the local gossip which tended to feature Freda Culham. But it was the sudden closing of Marion's banking account that brought Chief Inspector Karslake to Hillfoot on Friday morning. Adding Mrs. Harker's testimony of Marion Pinnaker leaving home in an overall and house shoes, Karslake was ready to explore the possibilities of The Floorboards Theory.

# Chapter Two

Karslake was invited to the most comfortable chair, nearest the electric stove. He was using his frank approach which was so often successful, perhaps because the frankness was genuine.

"It all adds up to what my missis would call queer goings-on. You've given contradictory explanations to different persons. We don't care tuppence about that. At this minute we're starting from scratch. Your wife disappeared on the afternoon of Tuesday the fifth. Will you begin there?"

"I'll have to start a bit further back." Pinnaker was rising to the occasion. "My wife and I had differences, but I did not want to break up. Let it be granted—I don't admit it, you understand—but let it be granted that I had given her cause to divorce me. She was very upset about it. Her religious views prevent her from entertaining the idea of divorce. In a nutshell, she said that she intended to desert me for the statutory three years. At the end of that time I could divorce her if I wished. If I preferred to resume our married life she would have had the three years in which to decide whether she would wish to do so."

"Plenty of others have done that," commented Karslake. "But she didn't have to run away and hide. It's legal desertion if she simply refuses to live under the same roof."

"She knew all that—she's a very knowledgeable woman. She insisted that it must be a genuine desertion, not a mere legal formula. She said she would go away in such a manner that I would not be able to find her. Her angle is that she has an inner need to change her way of living—sort of go into cold storage for three years. I knew it would be very awkward for me. For one thing, our financial arrangements are interlocked—"

"But why did she have to sneak out of the house? Without a change of clothes. Without even an overcoat."

"I just can't make it sound sensible!" Pinnaker was being frank, too.

"Any witnesses to the desertion story?"

"N-no—unless you count Marion herself as a witness." From his pocket case he produced the envelope addressed *Tom*. "I found it on the TV set when I came home that afternoon."

"The flap is stuck down," snapped Karslake.

"Yes—yes, it is!" Pinnaker was apologetic. "I may seem rather callous, but the fact is I had other things to attend to at the time and it slipped my memory. Perhaps you would prefer to open it yourself?"

Slipped his memory! A bit off-beat thought Karslake, as he thumbed the envelope open.

"'Dear Tom,'" he read aloud. "'At your request, I hereby put on record that I intend to desert you, in the moral as well as the legal sense, for the statutory period of three years. During that time I shall not communicate with you and shall make it impossible for you to communicate with me.'"

Karslake looked up. "That confirms her intention to desert you," he admitted.

"The next bit is more important, at the moment," said Pinnaker.

"'I cannot take seriously,'" read Karslake, "'your suggestion that you might be accused of murdering me. If such a fantastic thing were to happen, I would be certain to hear of it and you cannot believe that I would remain in seclusion and allow you to be convicted. Marion Pinnaker.'"

Karslake asked the obvious question:

"Did you dictate this letter?"

"I didn't actually dictate it. I wrote out the first paragraph for her, but I only made a note about the murder stuff. As a matter of fact, I added a bit about there being no ill-feeling on either side. I wish she had put that in."

Karslake blinked. Here was a frankness of heroic proportions. He studied the handwriting. It might be genuine. Pinnaker's tale might be true. In fact—a few hours later—the science department reported that the letter had not been forged.

"This letter," said Karslake, "answers all the questions before I've asked 'em. And tidies up all the loose ends—why she put all her money into Bearer Bonds, why she slipped away without anyone seeing her, why she took no clothes, not wanting to be traced through her luggage."

"Yes," said Pinnaker reflectively. "I think it does cover everything."

"Everything *except*—" Karslake reached for the ashtray "—when and how she left this house."

"Is that so important, Inspector?"

"Between you and me, Mr. Pinnaker, I don't suppose it matters a damn!" Karslake laughed and Pinnaker laughed too. "But as you probably know, we work by formula in these cases. Missing Wife. First thing: Has the husband salted her away under the floorboards? Yes—No. See what I mean?"

"Exactly!" chortled Pinnaker. "That's why I got her to write that letter." He was opening the door. "This house has an attic—you don't want to go up there, do you?"

"It's in the book," grinned Karslake. "Work downwards from roof to foundations."

The attics were a feature of these houses, as they were often required as extra rooms. On the upper landing Pinnaker stopped at a cupboard-like structure.

"Good lord, it's cold up here!" Pinnaker shivered. "I'm not sure I know how to work this thing. I've only been up there once—the week we moved in. We use the attic only for storage."

Karslake found the lever which opened the cupboard, where-upon a fanciful stepladder changed into position. Pinnaker went up and opened the trapdoor. Karslake followed. Conspicuous among a litter of household articles were two cabin trunks and three old suitcases, which proved to be empty.

Back on the upper landing, they contemplated five doors.

"The bathroom. The etcetera. And this is the guest room."

Karslake's eye was drawn to the bed by a gaudy coverlet barely covering the mattress which was evidently too big for it. When he went to the curtained recess he noticed an electric cord leading from an outlet in the wall to the mattress itself.

"The Allwhen mattress," exclaimed Pinnaker, the house-proud husband. "See that flex? It heats the mattress in winter. Nothing new in that. But look at this switch. Turn it to 'C' and a thermal unit draws out the air between the springs. Ventilates it: uses heat to make you cooler."

He whipped off the coverlet, laid himself full length on the bed, and would have expounded the hygienics of sleep if Karslake had been willing to listen.

The next room was smaller.

"Dressing room," said Pinnaker. "I'm sleeping in it now."

Pinnaker produced a bedroom key and unlocked the next door. "This is—was—our—her room."

Karslake noted twin beds stripped of bedclothes. Each was equipped with an Allwhen mattress, wired to a double outlet between the beds. He examined a wardrobe, a built-in cupboard, and a curtained corner, all containing clothes. As he flicked the curtain back, the draught dislodged a folded sheet of paper which had been lying flush with the skirting board.

"Looks like a bill," said Pinnaker.

"It's a railway ticket—bought on January second from an agent in Kingbiton—from Honshom to York, via London, first class. Journey dated for January fifth—last Tuesday. What d'you make of that, Mr. Pinnaker?"

"That she had planned beforehand to leave here on the Tuesday," answered Pinnaker. "But she cannot have planned to start at Honshom station in an overall and house shoes. Something went wrong with her plans. I can't understand it."

"I don't have to understand it—yet," said Karslake. "Anyway, she didn't go near Honshom station—we've checked."

Pinnaker re-locked the door before following the Inspector down the stairs.

"The sitting room you've seen. This is the dining room. The other is what we call my study. And there's the kitchen and scullery."

Karslake took the two living rooms first. In the kitchen he opened the cupboards, looked about, hesitated, then went through the scullery to the outhouse. The garden had been examined in Pinnaker's absence.

Back in the kitchen, Karslake pointed at the floor in the direction of the window:

"What's that?"

"I can't see what you're pointing at."

Karslake strode forward, then folded back the linoleum which was loose.

"Dammit, Inspector!" Pinnaker laughed grimly. "When you talked about putting wives under floorboards I thought you were joking."

"So did I!" said Karslake. "I didn't know then that these boards had been taken up. Look at that nail there—and this one."

"Oh, yes, I remember now!" exclaimed Pinnaker. "A little while ago we had a scare about dry rot."

"Good enough," said Karslake. "We'll check on the dry rot."

He went to the front door and whistled. Three men got out of the police car, one carrying a tool bag and the other a pick and spade.

Very shortly, Karslake joined Pinnaker in the sitting room.

"Found anything, Inspector?"

"It'll take them about half an hour. While we're waiting, you and I can pick up the loose ends."

Again the two men sat amicably by the stove. Karslake put a number of routine questions, watching Pinnaker for signs of strain. The answers were satisfactory, although Pinnaker invariably was unable to offer a witness.

"After you found your wife gone on Tuesday afternoon, did you leave the house before Wednesday morning?"

"Yes. And here at last I happen to have a witness—or rather, collateral evidence." Pinnaker passed an official-looking paper. "I found this waiting when I got home this evening. Summons for parking without lights at ten thirty that night—Tuesday, January fifth—at Shoreham. The Association will represent me and pay the fine."

"Shoreham-*on-Sea?*" said Karslake. "What might you have been doing at the seaside in the middle of a cold winter's night?"

"I don't know. I think I went there with the idea of—of drowning myself—"

He broke off as one of Karslake's men knocked and entered.

"No dry rot, sir. And nothing else. The whole area is undisturbed. Washout!"

"If I may butt in, Inspector," said Pinnaker, "would your staff be kind enough to put everything back? Mrs. Harker is a prickly customer."

"That's all right—we're all house-trained." When they were alone Karslake added, "You were telling me what you did at Shoreham-on-Sea.

Pinnaker looked unhappy.

"Forgive me, Inspector, but this does strike me as rather nightmarish. Floorboards are out of it, so we jump into my car and drive into a jungle of revolting possibilities. Did I dump my unhappy wife in the sea? If so the currents will probably bring her back, though we can't be certain about it, can we? In the hours of darkness I could have covered a large slice of country. The Sussex Downs, for instance—there are lots of dull corners no one ever visits. In Surrey, in the unbuilt parts of the Wey valley, there are innumerable, meaningless little ponds. Hampshire and Bucks are pockmarked with abandoned gravel pits. There are probably at least a hundred disused wells within fifty miles of this house—any one of which I might have used. I mean, your checking technique can hardly cover all that territory, can it?"

"Give the poor old technique a chance," Karslake was genuinely amused. "You tell me where you went in your car that night and I'll do my best to check it."

Pinnaker shook his head.

"Sorry, Inspector! I sincerely thank you for doing an unpleasant job in a thoroughly pleasant way. But, honestly, I've had enough of it. I propose to settle the whole matter myself by getting in touch with my wife."

"That certainly would settle it," admitted Karslake. "You think you can find her without our help?"

"*With* the help you've already given," corrected Pinnaker. "I'm sure I could interest a newspaper in this garish incident of the floorboards. And all that checking. And my journey after dark in the car. It will be clear to Marion that I am under suspicion and I am confident she will keep her word and come forward."

# Chapter Three

This chronicle can give no more than the barest outline of the publicity campaign, which stands by itself in the history of crime reportage and commentary. Its uniqueness lies in the fact that a man, suspected of murder, voluntarily discarded the protection afforded him by the law. Pinnaker told a conference of reporters that he wanted his wife to know that he was suspected of having murdered her. So he authorized them to work up all the facts in his disfavor and color them with the strong suggestion of guilt. He co-operated generously, refusing payment for his services.

In an open letter to Marion—front page, center—Pinnaker wrote:

*"After the police had torn up the floorboards in the kitchen and searched the foundations to see if I had buried you in the manner of Crippen, they asked me—very fairly—to account for a 'journey' in the car during the hours of darkness. It was no journey, Marion. It was a melancholy escape from the loneliness of what had been our home. I can remember only that I drove to the sea—I hardly know why. Everything else is a blank. There are many who believe that I threw your dead body into the sea, or disposed of it somewhere in the countryside."*

That may be taken as typical of the directly personal appeal he made in print and on the air. There was always just a touch of resentment in references to the floorboards incident. The rest was extremely fair-minded. The journey by night was the main feature. The sea would be dragged in, rather vaguely, without mention of Shoreham—emphasis being on the gravel pits and the disused wells. And always the moral was rubbed in—that there was such a strong *prima facie* case against Pinnaker that it was Marion's duty to come forward—alternatively the duty of anyone who had seen her to report to the police.

On Sunday the first sightseers came to gape at Hillfoot and wander into the garden, whereupon Pinnaker was given a police guard. The only personal friend to seek admittance was Freda Culham.

"This is wonderful of you—I shall never forget it!" exclaimed Pinnaker. "But I wish you had thought of yourself for once. The scandalmongers will make the most of your coming here."

"Darling! I'm in the scandal up to my neck. I'm The Other Woman in the Case—didn't you know? So let's be scandalous in comfort!"

"For one thing," persisted Pinnaker, "we should both feel rather awkward if Marion were to walk in while you're here."

There was a long silence before Freda said:

"Tom! On that Tuesday afternoon I was in this house with Marion until about a quarter to three."

"Good *lord!*" It was the first Pinnaker had heard of it. "She must have rushed out of the house as soon as you had left. Do the police know you were here?"

"I don't think anyone knows. I drove in and parked beside the garage." She then described her talk with Marion.

"A quarter to three!" exclaimed Pinnaker. "And yet you stand by me! Just like you—you refuse to believe that I killed her!"

She came close, put her hands on his shoulders. Perhaps at this moment it occurred to him that Freda was one of those women who make excellent mistresses but impossible wives.

"It would be all the same if I did believe you had killed her. She was playing dog-in-the-manger and deserved it. I hated her."

"You don't mean that, Freda! Not if I killed Marion!"

"Of course I mean it, silly boy! I don't know how soon we can get married, and it doesn't matter. When all this police business has blown over—"

"If you don't stop, I shall be sick." He pushed her away. "It's a perfectly revolting idea!"

The quarrel developed on conventional lines, leading to the conventional threat.

"It's the first time I've been thrown down, Tom, and it hurts. Aren't you afraid I might hit back?"

"No, darling!" He laughed. "Tell the police you were alone in the house with Marion—that she refused your demand for divorce and made you angry—a big strong woman like you who could tuck *her* under your arm. Tell them your car was parked next to the kitchen door. Tell them you left a few minutes before I entered the empty house."

She was so frightened that he had to water it down.

"I am only warning you that people may think you took her away in *your* car. It fits the facts. I am not suggesting you killed her—it's not your style. Besides, Marion is sure to come forward—probably tomorrow, certainly during the week."

But Marion did not come forward during the week—nor the week after.

Pinnaker, the home-lover, adapted his habits to circumstance. His attempt to economize on fuel had been abandoned after three days and the house was nearly as comfortable as ever, thanks to Mrs. Harker.

In the third week the publicity simmered down. Uninvited, he called on Karslake at Scotland Yard.

Karslake was not very genial.

"The ballyhoo has not produced your wife, Mr. Pinnaker."

"It has been a disappointment," confessed Pinnaker, "a humiliation! Some of my neighbors are cutting me. I shall have to resign from the committee of the tennis club. But I shall have one more try—on my own."

Karslake showed no curiosity.

"The newspapers," continued Pinnaker, "have written themselves dry—they have no new facts. Marion has not responded to facts. But she may respond to—sentiment. It was suggested to me that I should write a book—a history of our marriage and an appeal to Marion to return. Under the title *Marion, Come Back*. What do you think of the idea?"

"Nothing!" said Karslake. "The only advice I can give you, Mr. Pinnaker, is this: if you think of changing your address, be sure to let us know well in advance."

"There won't be any change of address. I shall have to stay in Honshom and live down the feeling against me—for the full period of three years. After all, my wife promised to come forward if I were in danger of *conviction*. Subject, of course, to your correction, Inspector—I am *not* in danger of conviction."

He was in no danger of conviction on the facts possessed by the police. In the next couple of months no new facts emerged, and the files subsided into the Department of Dead Ends ...

# Chapter Four

The Department of Dead Ends could reopen a case only at a tangent—when a ripple from one crime intersected the ripple from another. In May 1955—sixteen months after Marion Pinnaker's disappearance—Detective Inspector Rason was investigating a case of suspected arson in which, among many other things, an old Buick car had been burned out. The car's log had been burned too, but he was informed that the car had been bought second-hand from a Mr. Bellamy, who lived at Shoreham-on-Sea.

Mr. Bellamy confirmed the sale and added, "I myself bought it second-hand—from a man named Pinnaker. The man who was supposed to have murdered his wife. You remember? Just about the time it all happened, too."

That, thought Rason, was the sort of remark that often led to business. He went through the files of the Pinnaker case. The car sequence showed Pinnaker's admission of the drive by night—to Shoreham-on-Sea. Checked by Karslake on the summons for parking. Checked that the number of the car on the summons was that of a Buick car owned by Pinnaker. That tidied that up. What a pity!

Rason was putting the file away when he remembered to check the license numbers himself.

Number of the Buick car checked by Karslake: PGP421. Number of the burned out Buick: PGP421. The same car!

Nothing in that, thought Rason gloomily. Coincidence that Pinnaker should have happened to drive to Shoreham-on-Sea. Perhaps to clinch the sale of the car to Bellamy? In which case Bellamy might be able to throw some light on Pinnaker's movements that night. Just worth a ring on the chance of showing Chief Inspector Karslake he had missed something.

"Mr. Bellamy, sorry to trouble you again. On the night of Tuesday, January fifth, 1954, did Mr. Pinnaker drive in that Buick to see you at Shoreham?"

"No. I don't think he knows I live here—I dealt with him at his office. Anyhow, he couldn't have driven anywhere in that car on the Tuesday because he delivered it to me the previous day—Monday, the fourth."

Rason perceived only that there had been a tangle of dates.

"One more question if you don't mind, Mr. Bellamy. Did you have any trouble with the police over parking without lights that Tuesday night?—the fifth of January."

"It's funny you should ask. I did park without lights. And when I was going home I saw a chit fixed on the wiper, warning me that I would be reported. But I never got the summons. It just occurs to me, Mr. Rason, that Pinnaker may have got that summons. He delivered the car on Monday but I didn't receive the log from him until the Thursday, so the registration was still in his name."

Rason thanked him effusively. Already he was making wild guesses, all pivoting on his mental pictures of Freda Culham, Mrs. Harker, and Pinnaker himself, none of whom he had ever seen. He called at Pinnaker's office, posing as a prospective client. He was disappointed when he visited Freda Culham, who didn't seem to believe that he had once studied under her late father. And Mrs. Harker was very rude to him but unwittingly propped up the juiciest of his guesses.

The next step was to obtain Chief Inspector Karslake's consent to go ahead—usually a tricky business.

"You've got something there!" said Karslake, when Rason had told him the tale of the "two" cars. "But not very much!" he added in his most deflating style. "Pinnaker lied about the night ride. Maybe he didn't leave the house at all that night. That doesn't make him a killer."

"Let's try it the other way round," Rason was holding himself in. "You get a tip-off that Pinnaker may have scuppered his wife and buried her at home. You search the house and you find no stiff. O-kay! You're all smiles and apologies for troubling him. How does he react?"

"He didn't."

"Just so! When you tell Pinnaker he's in the clear, does he say 'cheers!'—like anybody else? No! He says, 'Mr. Karslake, don't be too sure I haven't murdered my wife, just because you found nothing under the floorboards! I went out for a long drive as soon as it was dark. How d'you know I didn't take the body along and dump it? He didn't use those words but that's what it adds up to. And now we know the midnight ride was a lie!"

"But not necessarily a killer's lie!"

"What's more," persisted Rason, ignoring the interruption, "Pinnaker flashed that parking summons to fake evidence that he had driven to the *sea!*"

"It doesn't surprise me as much as you'd think," said Karslake. "Take that letter the wife was supposed to have left behind for him. She wrote it herself, all right. But it was a darned funny letter. And that business about the way she was dressed—going out in winter in her indoor rig—that was darned funny too!"

"Which is the funny bit?" asked Rason.

"That book of his. Story of his married life—might have been almost anybody's married life. Yet it sold a half a million copies. And one of the Sunday papers printed about half of it in bits each week. Must have brought him thousands of pounds. He talks soft, but he's no softie."

Rason had missed the cash angle on the book. It took most of the wind out of his sails.

"Anything else?" asked Karslake.

"Mrs. Harker, for instance," said Rason with his customary irrelevance. "She's what I call a tower of strength. D'you know she nearly sacked herself because Pinnaker wouldn't let her use the furnace to keep the place warm? That was about the time when you made your examination of the house—sir!"

"Furnace? There was nothing in the furnace."

"Just so!" chirped Rason. "There was nothing in the furnace—when there ought to've been—*if* you understand me."

"I don't!" snapped Karslake. "One thing at a time! Tie him down on that car story of his and we'll charge him with creating a public mischief by misleading the police."

Pinnaker was making a very good job of living down the scandal. True, he could not appear at the tennis club, but a minority were ready to pass the time of day at a chance meeting. The police had left him unmolested. He had never been seen with Freda Culham and it was obvious that their friendship had ended. Mrs. Harker stood by him. Some believed that Marion would reappear at the end of the three-year period. His habits were as regular as ever except that he was frequently away from home on weekends. There were two sides to every question—and so on.

Pinnaker showed no recognition of Rason when the latter gave his name, but he greeted Karslake as an old acquaintance.

The police rarely have a personal animosity against a suspect unless he gives them personal cause. They accepted his offer of a drink. A little small talk passed. Then Rason opened—and in a manner that shocked his superior.

"A few days ago, Mr. Pinnaker, I talked to a Mr. Bellamy—the man who bought your old Buick. The short of it is we know now that your tale about going out after dark to Shoreham-on-Sea is all punk. You never left the house that night."

Karslake registered unease. Rason rippled on:

"That drive by night! Corpse in the car or *not*, according to taste! What was the idea, Mr. Pinnaker?"

"There was no idea—I acted on the spur of the moment. A childish impulse. And this is where I lose face." He made an appealing gesture which had no effect.

"Listen, please! It was obvious that Mr. Karslake believed me to be innocent of any criminal act. So when he started to search the house I did not take it seriously. To me, it was like a parlor game—I'll be the Murderer and you be the Detective! Without any effort, I began to identify myself with all the men who had murdered their wives and hidden their bodies. I tingled with fear. I felt guilty—in the sense that an actor can feel guilty while he is playing a murderer. I got a tremendous thrill out of it."

"Yes, but what about that car story?" pressed Rason.

"Wait! Mr. Karslake and I came downstairs. The whole experience was ending rather tamely—when Mr. Karslake spotted that the floorboards in the kitchen had been taken up recently. I told him about the dry rot—and he did not believe me! Quite suddenly, he saw me as a murderer who had concealed his wife's body under the floorboards. Floorboards, by heaven! Crippen! *Me!* It was wonderful! I had never felt so stimulated in my life. We sat in this room. Mr. Karslake asked me some questions to help him 'build up the case'—which I knew would be shattered in half an hour when the men found no body.

"Like a dope addict, I wanted more—and at once. I remembered that summons for parking—I knew it was intended for Bellamy—but I couldn't resist the temptation. With the summons to back up a car story I could go on playing the role of suspected man—living under a hanging sword that could never possibly fall. To you no doubt it sounds silly—perhaps even contemptible. I do not defend myself—and I suppose it's no good apologizing now."

Both Karslake and Rason had dealt with psychopaths who try to get themselves suspected for the sake of the thrill. Their silence encouraged Pinnaker to keep talking.

"My wife disappeared on the Tuesday afternoon, if you remember. By midday on Wednesday, Mrs. Harker's well-meant chatter had alerted half the neighborhood. If there had been a corpse in the house I couldn't possibly have moved it later than Wednesday morning—I couldn't have moved a dead rabbit without everybody knowing. Therefore I had to create suspicion of my actions on the Tuesday evening."

"So it was just a jolly prank!" exclaimed Rason. "Was Mrs. Pinnaker playing, too? That letter she wrote about coming forward if you were in danger? Was that part of the prank?"

"Certainly not!"

"We needn't go into that now," snapped Karslake.

"My superior officer," said Rason, nodding at Karslake, "is more interested in how and when Mrs. Pinnaker left this house. He won't tie you to that tale about her going away dressed in house clothes and nothing else but ten thousand quid in a brief case."

"To the best of my belief that is what she did."

"Come. Mr. Pinnaker! If she was excited or absent-minded she'd have been pulled up by the cold before she reached the gate. And if she was out of her mind and started walking away to nowhere, how far would she get in this suburb where pretty nearly everybody knows her? Dressed like that in January, she'd have been as conspicuous as if she'd been got up as a fan dancer. Yet no one saw her."

"I have nothing to add," said Pinnaker.

"Then I'll add a bit," retorted Rason. "Your wife did *not* leave the house that Tuesday. Something went wrong with your plans. And she didn't leave that Wednesday nor that Thursday nor that Friday. Your wife was in this house when my superior officer searched it!"

"You needn't answer that, Mr. Pinnaker," said Karslake. "It's ridiculous!"

Rason grinned at his senior. "Did you look under the beds—sir?"

Both men stared at him.

"Under the beds!" Rason repeated. "All those jokes about burglars under the bed—as if any burglar would be such a fool! It's such a damn silly place to hide anyone—living or dead—that when you come to think of it, it's rather a good place."

For a moment Karslake was doubtful.

"I was looking for a corpse—"

"And the corpse had to be under the floorboards!" cut in Rason.

"—I wasn't looking for a living woman. Come to that, she could have stayed in the attic while Mrs. Harker was here in the mornings. And dodged about while I was searching the house—"

"Could she? Let's try it—if Mr. Pinnaker doesn't mind."

Again they began with the attic. On the top landing, the built-in ladder clanged into position and clanged back again when Karslake decided that no woman, however slight, could have remained hidden in the attic.

"She couldn't have dodged from one room while I was in another and slipped up to the attic, because I would have heard that ladder." Glaring at Rason, he added, "If she *was* in this house when I searched it, she must have been in one of the rooms on this landing."

He opened the nearest door, which was that of the guest room.

"There you are! I didn't look under that bed because I can see under it from the doorway."

"Quite right!" agreed Rason, himself stepping into the room and examining the bed. "So this is the Allwhen mattress!" He observed the flex running from the mattress to an outlet in the wall. "Hot and cold laid on. Mrs. Harker told me about 'em—said they were unhealthy because—"

He was talking to himself. The others had inspected the smaller room and he joined them in the corridor.

"This is the big room," Pinnaker was saying. "It was—our room. It has not been in use since she left." The hint was not taken by Karslake. So Pinnaker produced a single key on a pocket chain, then opened the door.

The windows were shut and the room had a disagreeable mustiness. The twin beds were as Karslake had last seen them except for a slight film of dust. Pinnaker was chattering like an anxious host. He observed that Rason's eye was on one of the mattresses.

"That's the Allwhen mattress. By means of an insulated—"

"Yes, I've been told how they work," interrupted Rason and turned to Karslake.

"You've heard me speak of my niece—"

"Tell Mr. Pinnaker some other time," scowled Karslake.

"She's a fair-sized young woman. I measured her yesterday. Not for roundness—for thickness. Meaning the highest point of her when she's lying flat on the sitting-room floor. A shade over nine inches, she made."

He strode to the nearer bed, unfolded a pocket rule, and measured the sides of the Allwhen mattress.

"Ten inches thick," he announced. He folded the pocket rule. "Mrs. Pinnaker was a small woman, wasn't she?"

"Five foot three—and slender," answered Pinnaker.

"Small enough to fit easily inside one of these mattresses—in which case Mr. Karslake would probably have missed it, having his mind on floorboards."

"I don't think a skilled eye could be deceived—nor even an unskilled one," said Pinnaker indulgently. "If you remove the springs and the insulation and the cold air conduit, you have little more than a canvas bag. The silhouette of a human being—"

"There'd be no silhouette if she'd been packed in nicely by a skilled upholsterer. When you were a youngster at Bettinson's, Mr. Pinnaker, you learned upholstery, didn't you?"

"True!" answered Pinnaker. "But the most skilled upholsterer in the world could not prevent a corpse enclosed in such a mattress from declaring its presence after a day or two."

"That's right!" cried Karslake. "If there had been a corpse in one of the mattresses that evening, I couldn't have helped knowing it. But I'll own up I'd have missed a *living* woman!"

"A living woman sewn up in a mattress?" asked Pinnaker.

"Sewn up or buttoned up by a skilled upholsterer an hour before I arrived. That mattress has about a dozen air vents—and you could have prepared it weeks beforehand."

Pinnaker looked thoughtful

"Physically possible, I suppose," he conceded. "But what on earth *for!* What would be the purpose of such a trick—which, as you say, must have been planned beforehand?"

Karslake answered the question with another.

"How many thousands did you make on that book of yours, Mr. Pinnaker—*Marion, Come Back?*"

Pinnaker caught his breath.

"You used Mrs. Harker pretty smartly," continued Karslake. "You two did some conjuring tricks with those clothes. You gave Mrs. Harker faked evidence. So she told us in good faith that tale about your wife going away in her house clothes—which made it dead certain the police would come here and search the house for a corpse. You played up the newspapers and the TV, as you played up Mrs. Harker. And now you're going to tell me that as a result of all that advertisement no one was more surprised than yourself when half a million suckers bought that book!"

"Suckers!" echoed Pinnaker. He flushed and his voice revealed an unsuspected aggressiveness. "Let me tell you something! That book may have had its faults from a literary angle. But the public liked it. They bought it—they passed it from hand to hand—and they talked about it. And you have the damned effrontery to call them *suckers!*"

Rason stepped between them. Karslake regarded Pinnaker with some surprise.

"I apologize for saying 'suckers'," he said coldly. "But you admit that the two of you hoaxed us—as well as the newspapers?"

"Absolute rot!" stormed Pinnaker. Then with sudden calm he continued, as if repeating a prepared statement: "I admit only that I personally misled the police with that car story. I expect to be prosecuted for having 'created a mischief.' I deny that my wife helped me in any way whatever. Alternatively, if she did help me, she did so 'under the domination of her husband.' You can't touch her."

"Good enough!" snapped Karslake. "It's your case, Rason. You can take his statement."

When Karslake had left the house Rason rejoined Pinnaker in the sitting room.

"This statement will take some time, won't it?" suggested Pinnaker, producing a portable typewriter. "Let's have another drink before we start?"

"Not for me, thanks!" Rason's tone carried a reminder of duty to be done. "Never mind the typewriter. What about that furnace of yours? The one that heats the house."

Pinnaker smoothed the hair from his forehead.

"Your senior got my goat, Mr. Rason. I'm finding it hard to concentrate. If you won't join me, d'you mind if I have a drink by myself?"

He opened the cocktail cabinet. His back was toward Rason but his face was reflected in a glass panel of the bookcase.

"At the time, Mr. Pinnaker, you were hard pressed for a thousand pounds. Saving a trifle on house fuel wouldn't have helped you. You let the fire out on that Tuesday night. You kept it out during Wednesday and Thursday. But on Friday—after the house had been searched for the dead body of your wife—you lit the fire again and heated the house."

"In a crisis one's small acts are sometimes idiotic." Pinnaker's face showed indifference but Rason was watching his hands, reflected almost as clearly as if the glass panel had been a mirror.

A second later Rason crept up like a cat and snatched the half-filled tumbler of whisky.

"What's that you dropped in the glass?"

"Only a sedative. I told you Karslake had rattled me."

"Then it wouldn't do me any harm." Rason raised the glass to his lips.

"If you drink that it will kill you," said Pinnaker calmly. "I don't think you intend to drink it, but I daren't take the risk."

"Good boy!" said Rason. There was a long silence while he opened his bag, poured the contents of the glass into a small bottle, then shut the bag. "There's not much of the murderer about you, Mr. Pinnaker. When she wouldn't let you have that thousand you lost your temper and dotted her one. Didn't you? I'm just guessing."

"You are! All you've got is that I tried to kill myself," said Pinnaker. "How much do you *know?*"

"Enough to go on guessing," chirped Rason. "After you had given her that unlucky wallop on Tuesday afternoon, you put her in the attic, out of Mrs. Harker's way. You kept the house close to freezing for obvious reasons. You had plenty of time to doctor that mattress and get her sewn up inside before the Chief Inspector came on Friday evening. And you messed about with the floorboards, so's he'd be certain to have 'em up. Then everybody would be sure that there was no corpse in the house. Am I right?"

"As there are no witnesses present—yes, you are substantially right." Pinnaker thrust his hands into his pockets as if he did not trust them. "But you still have no evidence. After that Friday, I was able to use my other car without anyone suspecting that it might contain a corpse—and so was able to hide it in the countryside—"

"No good, laddie!" interrupted Rason. "The safest place in the world to hide that corpse was the one place where Chief Inspector Karslake had reported that there was no corpse!"

Under the floorboards, deeply buried, the police found the body of Marion Pinnaker, clothed in sweater, skirt, and overall—beside the body a pair of thin blue house shoes and an attaché case containing ten thousand pounds in Bearer Bonds.

*A Woman of Principle*

# Chapter One

Margaret Whinley's mother, a widow, was a crank, publicly disowned by the Movement which she was held to discredit by her excesses—namely the Movement to abolish the death penalty. This was, of course, long before the Homicide Act of 1957.

From the age of seven, Margaret was not infrequently kept from school to wait outside a prison in the early morning, the purpose being not ghoulish but propagandist. With a handful of others her mother would weep a little, bluster a little, and distribute pamphlets, produced at her own expense. Then they would return to their comfortable home in the suburbs, which was normal except for the ever-growing pile of pamphlets on the hall table which emphasized the physical and psychological horrors of a judicial execution, with illustrations—quite a lot of illustrations.

The reason for Margaret's absences became known at school. Whether she was envied or pitied, she was labeled "odd"—which she was not. She escaped unpopularity but could make no close friends. In adolescence she was withdrawn, a little self-righteous and inclined to talk like a governess. She never read about crime nor discussed it of her own free will. Deep down in her was implanted a conviction that to hang a murderer was itself a form of murder. It was more than an opinion—a first principle, the kind of thing one need never discuss.

When Margaret was twenty-two her mother died, leaving a small capital sum which yielded less than the girl's salary as a first-class typist. Good luck enabled her to obtain a suitable flat, but she soon found that living alone was too much for her. She invited Eileen Revers to share her flat.

Eileen came from the West country—the only one of a large family to prefer town life. They were of the same physical type—each a little taller than the average, with lithe, well-formed bodies and good coloring—a couple of unobtrusively good-looking girls.

A warm friendship grew up, giving Margaret something she had wanted and needed all her life. For two years, working for the same company, they were content with each other and untroubled by problems of their future. They had individual interests which they shared in chatter. No confidences were withheld—until Eileen fell in with James Grantham.

Eileen's love story follows a familiar pattern of disaster. At the beginning, she told Margaret everything she felt about him, though she never mentioned how and where she had met him. His parents, she said, were in Washington, his father being a minor embassy official. James was, himself, she said, "connected with" the diplomatic service—which meant, she further explained, that he had very interesting work, with the drawback that he could never quite call his time his own.

Like Eileen herself, Margaret swallowed it whole. Margaret knew surprisingly little about men—she had no brothers, not even any male cousins. A few noncommittal kisses at parties had taught her less than nothing.

James Grantham became one of the interests that were shared in chatter. Margaret enjoyed the very nearly secret anecdotes "connected with" the diplomatic service. Her interest was so sympathetic that, in a sense, she shared Eileen's lover. She could imagine herself in Eileen's place, sitting with a shadowy James Grantham in the modest little restaurant, or at the cinema, perhaps holding hands.

Quite often, she dreamed of this man whom she had not yet seen.

At first delightful, it soon became intolerable.

"Eileen!" Margaret had shattered one of the anecdotes about James Grantham. "I've heard so much about him that I feel I know him quite well. I must meet him! Bring him here to supper on Saturday night, and I'll put up cold chicken and a sherry trifle."

She went on: "And we ought to keep some gin on the premises. I'll see to that."

Margaret bought a dress for the occasion. But there was no occasion. Eileen came home unattended because James Grantham, she said, had been suddenly required to go on duty. The diplomatic service was like that. You never knew. Margaret took it, nearly, at its face value. Weeks slipped by with little change.

About the end of March, though Eileen had never announced that he had proposed marriage, the chatter veered to homemaking, with special reference to a wife whose husband could not keep regular hours.

Margaret once more invited Eileen to bring him to supper—this time suggesting a date a fortnight hence, with alternatives. But, in the event, Eileen again became the mouthpiece of his regrets.

"I know it looks rude to you, Margaret, and it's a bit thick for me. But it's awful for Jim! He had been looking forward to coming, and he nearly *cried* when he found at the last minute that he couldn't make it."

"It's all right, darling!" Margaret didn't believe that Grantham had nearly cried. For one disloyal instant she was ready to doubt whether he had ever received the invitation. The governess element in her had taken charge.

"Eileen, have your people ever met him?"

"It's been too difficult to fix anything. If he had ordinary office hours—"

"*Quite so!* Don't you think, dear, that in fairness to yourself and those who care for you—"

"If you'll let me finish—Mother and Dad have asked him to stay for the first fortnight in June. I've arranged to take my holiday then, and we shall go down together."

There were no more anecdotes and no more chatter about homemaking, but Margaret barely noticed the change. Her mental picture of James Grantham was unaffected by his odd behavior in the matter of invitations. His shadow continued to beckon her to imaginative adventure.

# Chapter Two

In the first week in June, Eileen set off with an affectionate, almost tearful farewell. Ten days later, when Margaret returned from the office, she found Eileen in the living room.

"Darling! Is it really you?"

Eileen was sitting upright, unnaturally still, and unresponsive.

"I've made a fool of myself, Margaret . . . Jim . . ." Eileen looked tired, almost haggard.

"Don't get up," insisted Margaret, "I'll get you some tea."

"Not tea! We've still got that gin, haven't we?"

Margaret produced the bottle which had been bought for James Crantham.

"I told you a lie about our going to see my parents. We're at a beach bungalow at Thadbourne. We've been lovers for months."

The cork slipped from Margaret's hand. While she picked it up, she felt embarrassment—as if it were she herself who had made the confession.

"And now you've had a row and he's left you?"

"No, he hasn't. We haven't even had the row—yet! He doesn't know I know a thing. He's up here in London today and he'll be back before midnight. I'm going down on the 7:10, and I shall be the one to make the row."

"Do you think, dear, one can ever be justified in—"

"Diplomatic service, he told me, but I had my suspicions weeks ago. His yarns began not to add up. After he'd gone this morning, I happened to put my hand in his dressing-gown pocket."

Eileen rummaged in a shopping bag and brought out an envelope, from which she drew a headed memo slip.

"'Eshelby & Co., Sanitary Manufacturers Agents, 51, Blucher Street, London, E.1.'" Margaret read aloud. "'Please meet me at Customs' office at 11:30 a.m. Wednesday 12th inst., with van Rijnder's invoice vis. 500 Lavatory Basin Bracket Size B.'"

"Diplomatic service!" exclaimed Eileen. "Diplomatic not to mention it to your friends!" She replaced the slip in the shopping bag. "I don't care what a man's job is as long as it's straight. *Somebody* has to sell—sanitary fittings! But if one lie, why not another? What about his father in Washington? And besides that—for all I know, he—he may have a wife!"

There had been a note of dread in the last words which puzzled Margaret.

"But you don't want to marry a man who tells you snobbish little lies." As Eileen stared, Margaret plunged on. "I know you think I'm a prude but I'm not. I don't see anything very dreadful in living with a man you think you love—provided, of course—"

"*Provided of course!*" echoed Eileen. After a long pause she went on. "If there isn't a wife, he'll have to marry me right away. I don't mind, really. I do still love him, sort of, and I could manage him into making something of himself."

She enlarged on the theme of rebuilding James Grantham until she had to dash for her train.

Half an hour later, Margaret found the shopping bag which Eileen had left behind. She examined the contents. Drapers' parcels and two glass jars of delicatessen. She came upon the envelope containing the memo—hating it as the instrument of exposure. Eileen had made too much of the deception. After all, it was only a form of show-off, harmless in itself. She would not enclose the envelope with the draperies—it might reveal to Grantham that Eileen had rifled his pockets. On the other hand, Eileen might wonder whether she had left it lying about.

*Dear Eileen*, she wrote, *I thought you might be needing the things you bought, so am forwarding them herewith, except the glass jars. I am keeping your note about the sanitary fittings until we meet again—which I hope will be soon—with lots of good news.—Margaret.*

She put the envelope containing the memo into her purse, for return to Eileen at their next meeting—then posted the parcel, addressed to *Mrs. Grantham.*

By the following afternoon, when the news broke, Margaret was able to persuade herself that she had had a premonition of disaster—that she had "known" she had been speaking to Eileen for the last time. Certainly the fact of Eileen's death brought tears, but no great shock of surprise. That death should come to her by manual strangulation seemed to have a logic of its own. Eileen had probably maddened him with her taunts.

She studied the report in the evening papers. It was the same as all those other crimes—crimes of passion, Mother used to call them. (*You'll understand it better when you're older.*) She was older now and did understand it. ( ... *they really do see red—they're sick men, not responsible for their actions—so if we have breakfast at half-past six, dear, we shall be at the prison in nice time.*)

Her eye slid off the photograph of Eileen to one of an elderly woman, a Miss Stanmore, owner of the bungalow. She had personally let it to Grantham, who had paid a month's rent in cash. She had not taken references as the couple had seemed so thoroughly respectable.

The return address on the parcel brought the police to the flat in quest of a photograph of Grantham.

"I've never seen one—I've never even seen him," said Margaret. "That was her room, if you'd like to search it."

When they failed to find a photograph they searched the flat, at Margaret's invitation, on the chance of a mislaid letter, or even an envelope.

"There was an old portable typewriter at the bungalow." Detective-Inspector Curwen showed her a specimen of its writing, indicating a misalignment, but she could give no help. To the best of her belief, Grantham had never written to Eileen.

"Any idea what his job was, Miss Whinley?"

"I know he told her he was in the diplomatic service. But she had discovered it wasn't true. She had found him out in other lies and she was very unhappy. That's why she came here yesterday and confessed to me she was living with him."

When the detective had gone Margaret, happening to open her purse, caught sight of the envelope containing instructions concerning the lavatory basin brackets.

"Funny I didn't think of it when he asked me what Grantham's job was. I wonder what I ought to do?" She knew what the law required her to do—join in the hunt. (*The pitiful spectacle of a half-demented creature trying to outwit the intelligence and organized might of the police.*)

She shifted her compact and her comb and her handkerchief on top of the envelope so that she need not see it every time she opened her bag.

It was a popular murder. There was the previous innocence and respectability of the victim—attested by Margaret in an interview extracted from her on the pavement as she was leaving for the office; there was the description of Grantham which fitted thousands—the man sitting next to you on the underground; there was the ambivalent hope that the hunted man would keep running and that he would be caught.

Margaret, who had offered no material evidence, was not required to attend the inquest. After the funeral, Eileen's parents called on Margaret, who told them all they wished to know.

Mrs. Revers asked all the questions. She began by putting herself at unnecessary pains to explain that she did not hold Margaret responsible, but she ended by saying that events might have taken a different course if Eileen's parents had been warned of the attachment to an obviously undesirable man.

"That's nonsense," said Mr. Revers, speaking almost for the first time. "Miss Whinley asked the man here and he wouldn't come. You couldn't expect her to sneak on her friend. In the hall, as they were leaving, he summed up. "I shall pray that man gets caught and hanged. It's not vengeance—not altogether. As long as he's at large, he may kill another poor girl who trusts him."

The words lingered with Margaret. Grantham might kill another girl. That was an aspect of murder which had not been emphasized in the pamphlets dealing with the horrors of judicial execution.

After the inquest, The Bungalow Murder began to fade out of the news. *The Reflector* summarized it as an unsolved mystery, pointing out that the police had nothing to work on. At Thadbourne, a number of persons had noticed the girl and the fact that she had a male companion; but only one person—the elderly lady who owned the bungalow—had spoken to him and she alone could positively identify him. Most probably he had resumed his identity as a respectable citizen and would never even be suspected.

And if he is never even suspected, Margaret reflected, he may kill some other poor girl who trusts him. She had suppressed evidence which might have resulted in arrest ... It was wrong to hang a man: therefore it must be wrong to procure his hanging. Reason evaporated in fantasy. (*I'll get to the prison in nice time. Listen to me, everybody! That man would be alive now, but for me. I handed him over to be hanged!*)

For a week the conflict tore her. Then she plucked up courage to take out the compact and the comb. The envelope was lying flat uppermost. She stared at it until the spell was broken. Then she picked it up and turned it over.

The address was printed, which seemed wrong somehow. It was stamped but the stamp had not been cancelled. She read again the typed memo slip and observed a misalignment. It was initialled. The initials were decipherable as J.E.—presumably J. Eshelby.

"Grantham" had not received that memo by post. The unused stamp and the printed London address! It must have been "Grantham" who had intended to post the memo—to instruct a subordinate—after typing it on the portable in the bungalow. Therefore, "Grantham" was Eshelby. Or he might be only Eshelby's manager. Awkward. One could not walk up to a man and ask him if he happened to be a murderer.

By the middle of the morning she was crossing London to the East End. Blucher Street, a blind alley ending at the river embankment, had been a residential terrace. Half of it had been bombed and was now a car park. The surviving half consisted of three-story houses mainly used for business. Entering No. 51, she opened a door on her left, labelled *Inquiries.*

The one-time front room and dining room had been converted into one and was now a combined office and storeroom. A girl in a loud jumper was fitting the cover over a typewriter. She looked at Margaret with annoyance.

"It's five to twelve and we're shutting till Monday."

"Will you please take this note to Mr. Eshelby and say that I will wait for the answer?"

The girl grudgingly took the envelope and went upstairs with it. Inside the envelope was a half sheet on which Margaret had written her name and address in full. If Eshelby were Grantham it would be enough. If he were not, no harm would be done.

"Mr. Eshelby says will you go up, please. It's the first door you come to, top of the stairs. The front door will be shut when you come down, but it'll open on the latch. There! It's striking twelve—I'm off."

The front door was slammed, leaving hall and staircase to be illumined by the fanlight only. While Margaret moved cautiously to the staircase she recited Miss Stanmore's description: height about five foot nine, age about 30, cleanshaven, nose straight, regular features, eyes large and brown, deep voice.

She was nearly at the top of the stairs when a door opened.

"This way, Miss Whinley. I'm sorry that girl has no manners."

The voice was deep; the height was about five feet nine, which was her own; the features were regular and the eyes were brown.

"Thank you," she said as he bowed her into a well-furnished office and drew back a padded swivel chair.

Margaret was struggling to readjust her ideas. She had no doubt that this man was "Grantham"—the murderer! She had assumed that "the brand of Cain" must have some kind of literality. She had expected at least the human equivalent of the doubtful sort of dog that looks as if it might bite you.

This man looked remarkably like the shadow she had summoned on many a lonely evening. She would never forgive him for that. If anything, he was better-looking than she had imagined.

"Well now, Miss Whinley, will you tell me what I can do for you?"

Margaret opened her purse and took out the envelope.

"She found this in your dressing-gown pocket."

He did not ask who "she" was. He glanced at the memo, then nodded and smiled vacuously.

"It's all Greek to me, Miss Whinley. Haven't you come to the wrong address?"

"Miss Stanmore will know," answered Margaret.

She wished she had not spoken so bluntly—she blamed herself for tearing away the decencies. She had thumped the bluff out of him. She wished he would say something or make some sound. His lower lip was stretched, like that of a child about to howl. This was The Hunted Man of all the pamphlets. She had always thought of something tragically gallant—forgetting why the hunted man was being hunted.

"Forgive me." He was trying to build up a front. "I never guessed it could happen like this—without the police." He covered his face with his hands. "Don't worry—I won't try and bolt out at the back. I'll come with you to the police. But we don't need Miss Stanmore, blowing off her grievances. Can't we give her the slip?"

"She isn't here."

He dropped his hands and sat upright.

"You didn't bring her along? And you haven't been to the police!—they wouldn't have let you come here."

As clearly as if he had put it into words she knew he had realized that he and she were alone in that house.

She watched him slide out of his chair and edge round the corner of the table towards her. She held her head back, as if to offer her throat. But the exquisite moment of mortal fear eluded her. With reason or without, she could feel no fear of this man. Their eyes met, hers reflecting disappointment.

"You haven't enough nerve left, have you?"

"You're laughing at me." The deep voice thinned to a querulous whimper. "Anyhow, I bet you've got *someone* outside!"

"And if I hadn't and you'd murdered me, you'd have had to run away afterwards—and then you would stand no chance at all."

"What chance do I stand now?"

"I don't know. Go back to your chair and we'll see." For the first time in her life the governess-tone was effective. Here was someone who would listen to her and obey. "Why did you kill Eileen?"

"That's a funny sort of question!" He blinked. "I don't know. It began with her saying there was a kid coming along and we'd got to get married. And I said how did I know it was mine."

"That was a silly insult. You know she loved you madly."

"Madly!" he scoffed. "But the wrong kind of mad. It was fine at first. She was full of fun and games, and so was I. Just the two of us. As a matter of fact, you spoiled all that."

"When I'd never seen you and really knew nothing about you? How could I?"

"Asking me to supper. The wrong idea altogether. It started her thinking. Home and respectability, and all that. First thing I really noticed was when she started saving money. My money, I mean. Wouldn't let me spend anything on her. Doing everything on the cheap. Rather sit in the park than go to a show. Wanted us to go to cheaper hotels. I was beginning to get cold feet, but she wouldn't let go. I'd given her an accommodation address, and she'd keep writing and 'phoning and wiring. I thought she might snap out of it if we had a few weeks together, so I took that bungalow. You know it all now."

"No, I don't," said Margaret. "If you found her as attractive as you did, why couldn't you marry her? Have you a wife living?"

"Not me—I'm not the marrying sort. I like to put in steady work here, then have a bit of fun outside with the girls. I thought Eileen felt the same—until she let me see that the fun was only the bait. Cor! Coming home every evening to the same woman and seeing her first thing every morning—year after year! I couldn't do it, Miss Whinley. See what I mean?"

If Margaret did not see what he meant, she sensed that he was telling a truth about himself.

"And for those reasons you decided to rob her of her life?"

"I didn't *decide* anything! She started a row. You'd be surprised at the cruel things she said—a refined girl like that. Dragged in the diplomatic service—a bit of moonshine I cooked up so I could do myself justice. I'm romantic. My business is not—the way a girl looks at it. I had to shut her up, and somehow I found I'd got her by the throat. That sort of settled it. Seemed at the time as though it was a case of her life or mine. Felt I couldn't turn back once I'd started. If I'd had the sense to say to myself, 'Stop, you fool, you'll kill that girl in a minute,' I'd have stopped. Do you believe what I'm telling you?"

"I suppose I do. Eileen deliberately made you angry. You got her taunts all mixed up with the marriage you did not want, and you whipped yourself into an hysteria in which you felt compelled to kill. When you came to your senses, you were horrified."

"That's right," cried Eshelby. "Thank God I've convinced you!"

"Thank God you've convinced me," echoed Margaret, "that the whole thing is likely to happen again with the next poor girl who trusts you and then has to tell you that it's your belated duty to marry her."

"Not after what I've been through!"

"You would have escaped if you had happened to post that memo as you intended. And then you would have experienced nothing that could make you suffer. Next time, you would simply be more careful." She added, "There will be no next time."

She got up—intending, as she believed, to go to the police. On her way across the room, the floor seemed to swing gently, threatening her balance. (*No, dear, it is NOT an eye for an eye and a tooth for a tooth. The poor wretch has to wait three Sundays, counting the days, the hours, the minutes.*)

She turned back and the floor steadied under her feet. She went to his side of the table, towered over him hunched in his chair.

(*What these tragic invalids need is treatment, inspired by understanding. Of course, no one suggests that they should retain their full liberty.*)

"Fear makes you wish that you had married Eileen, though you hate the idea of marriage. You now have the choice of marrying *me* or being hanged."

"Well, I'm damned!" He was startled out of his fear. "You want to marry—me?"

"No more than I want to hang you!" she flashed. "Try hard to understand—it's *you* who have thrust this ghastly choice on *me*. Marrying you is the only way of *not* hanging you."

He was near to gibbering with bewilderment and anxiety.

"Listen, I'll do anything! But I don't get it! Where do you come in? What've I got to do?"

"You'll have to show by your life from now on that it's wrong to hang men like you." Her answer seemed incomplete. She added, "There is, of course, no question of—mutual attraction. It will be a marriage of penance—on both sides."

"Penance?" he repeated.

The governess element in Margaret rose to its peak moment.

"Let it be clearly understood that there will be no more—'girls'—for you. Morally, you are a backward child, in need of treatment. I shall try to make you grow up. Whether I succeed or fail, you will never be given the chance to murder anyone else—until you have murdered me."

It was theatrical and it was pretentious, but it was none the less sincere. She believed that she was dedicating her life to her principles—failing to take warning from James Eshelby's remarkable resemblance to the dream lover with whose shadow she had spent so many lonely evenings at the flat.

# Chapter Four

James Eshelby, of course, was in no position to raise objections. When he learned that Margaret intended to remain financially self-supporting, he could hardly believe his luck. Unless a fairly large photograph of himself were published in the papers and Miss Stanmore happened to see it, he was in no danger, provided Margaret kept her word. They were to be married in a month. There were worse things. She hadn't the touch of glamour that Eileen had, but she was not bad-looking, and her figure was every bit as good. She had been almost matey when discussing the four empty rooms in the house.

That stuff she had handed him about not being attracted! If she hadn't fallen for him, it didn't make sense.

Margaret began the process of vacating her flat and selling her furniture. She had already resigned her job and changed her bank. James Eshelby, she decided, must not meet any of her small circle—it would be morally indecent. She had no thought of evading the police. Being wholly ignorant of police technique, she believed that the search for "Grantham" had been abandoned as hopeless. She registered as "Mrs. Eshelby" at an agency supplying temporary secretaries.

During the month she added sociability to the list of virtues essential to her task. A woman could not help a man to remodel his character by constantly glowering at him. In the middle of the first week she invited him to dinner at a Soho restaurant. He turned up well-groomed, cheerful, and attentive—a very different man from the craven to whom she had dictated the terms on which he would be allowed to live. Before she realized what she was saying she told him that she had enjoyed herself.

They had as many practical plans to discuss as a normal couple and James Eshelby discussed them normally. He interested her in the mechanism of his agency. He told her business yarns that were nearly as adventurous as if they had been about the diplomatic service. There were stretches of minutes which lent substance to her one-time dreams of the shadowy lover she had shared with Eileen. Afterwards, she would lie awake questioning herself. The overall answer was that it cannot be wrong to enjoy yourself while engaged in acts of self-sacrifice. So it could not be wrong to laugh at his jokes. He was very good at creating little jokes that were funny only to the two of them.

His house awakened her interest. It seemed to grow larger as she became more familiar with it At the third visit she discovered a sizeable back yard, bounded by a brick wall with a narrow door giving on to a back street. It contained a modern twenty-foot shed which he said was his 'warehouse.' She noted that goods would have to be brought by hand through the narrow door.

Three days before their wedding, she made a final inspection of the decorations.

"That paint comes up nicely," she approved. "And you were right about the bathroom. Everything is better than I expected."

"That's how it's going to be from now on." His tone drew her eyes to him. "I've known it for the last three days." She was silent, but she did not turn away. He came closer. "I've never called you by your name before. I'm going to, now. Listen . . ."

He had used that little tag on many previous occasions, and his timing was good. While she was being kissed, Margaret enjoyed an ecstatic vision of herself as the symbol of James Eshelby's repentance. She was his Second Chance, herself a steppingstone to—this-that-and-the-other.

# Chapter Five

They had planned to come straight home to the house in Blucher Street. After the ceremony at the registrar's, however, Margaret allowed him to whisk her off to Brighton for a weekend honeymoon.

The police, of course, had not abandoned their search for "Grantham." They were working backwards on the habits and ascertainable movements of Eileen, hoping to make a contact. Needing some further information, Inspector Curwen sought Margaret's help, arriving at her flat at a time when Margaret herself was on the train to Brighton.

Miss Whinley, the caretaker said, had left no forwarding address, but he knew where her furniture had been sold by auction. The auctioneer in turn knew only the address of the flat—she had collected her money from him in person. Later, the company that had employed her could help only with the address at which she had lived with her mother—which proved a dead end.

Margaret Whinley was no crook; but, reflected Inspector Curwen, she had bolted as a crook bolts. Why? If she had run off with a married man there would be no need for this elaborate cover-up. She had been unable to give him the slightest help in the matter of Grantham. She had not seen him, didn't know what his job was, nor any single thing about him. Or did she? Put it how you like, it was at least a long shot that if they could find the Whinley girl they would find the man who had murdered her best friend. Curwen was as nearly shocked as is possible for so experienced a detective.

At Brighton, Margaret was whirling herself off her feet. Eshelby was always able to abandon himself to the mood of the moment, detaching himself from his past and ignoring his future. That weekend closely approached Margaret's own conception of what a honeymoon ought to be. In the months that followed it would have been difficult to define in what way this marriage of penance differed from the ordinary marriage of a couple well pleased with one another.

The secretarial agency provided a succession of well-paid temporary jobs. They would dine out and go on to an entertainment, or spend a contented evening at home. Jim was attentive, amusing, companionable. The "ghastly choice" that had been thrust upon her was losing its ghastliness. Into the mental and emotional fog came a patch of light. She was not leading the dedicated life, as she had intended; she had married the murderer of her best friend—and was in danger of living happily ever afterwards.

A murderer was in need of treatment, the pamphlets had insisted, but they had given no definition of that magic word. Treatment, presumably, of his murderous impulse, of his morbidity, of his inability to control his passions. Jim's conduct, however, proved irreproachable. Or perhaps it only seemed so. Was she lacking in vigilance? In the working week he spent fourteen hours out of the twenty-four in her company. There were the remaining ten during which Miss Howes, his typist, was accessible. Margaret's path seemed clear.

"Jim, I want you to get rid of Miss Howes. There's nothing she does for you that I can't do better. And I'd like to help you."

"That's a most generous offer," he said, with superb self-control. "Only, I'm afraid it wouldn't work out. She knows the routine backwards."

"Then it must be a very simple routine! I'll start with you on Monday. You can begin to show me the routine over the weekend."

That, really, was all that was said on the point of sacking Miss Howes. For the first time, if only by her tone of voice, she had reminded him of the existence of Miss Stanmore.

After a meditative silence, he said, "You don't think there's been any funny business with that girl, do you? I mean—I may be a fool, Margaret—but I thought you and I were getting along all right."

"I have nothing to complain of, Jim, but I think that some decisions must rest with me."

She saw him flush and repress a retort, but thought that the reminder would be good for him.

As his secretary and deputy, Margaret saved him time and helped his judgment. When he left the office, she kept tabs on his movements. This increased efficiency, but it made Eshelby feel like a dog on a leash.

After a month of it, he took his courage in both hands. He mentioned the name of an American company, whose representative was crossing on the *Queen Mary*.

"I thought I'd run down to Southampton tonight and meet him."

Margaret turned the pages of *The Times*.

"The *Queen Mary* is not due until seven tomorrow evening. We can go down after lunch tomorrow."

"*We!*" He was horrified. "A man can't tote a wife along to a business talk!"

"You can explain that I'm your secretary."

"It would make him laugh! All right, the Southampton idea is off. I suppose I haven't been 'in' long enough to be let out for twenty-four hours on parole."

When he had left the room, Margaret pondered the taunt, discovering a retrospective sting in its tail. Was it possible that he was feeling their marriage as a prison sentence, while she had deluded herself that they were enjoying an unexpected happiness?

She knew the answer very soon. After the Southampton incident he ceased to pursue her attention and evaded all favors. She faced the fact that he had no personal interest in her whatever. In short, for a few months she had been one of his "girls"—of whom he had now tired and had lost the power of pretending otherwise. So be it!

The existence of Miss Stanmore gave Margaret total control on all major issues. But it was altogether too formidable a weapon for everyday use. She needed something more flexible—something which contained, as it were, the possibility of graded punishment.

Punishment for murdering Eileen? Hardly! Punishment for scorning Margaret? That question was not raised.

"It seems to me, Jim, that your business is little more than a collecting agency. Surely you would do better if you were to *buy* from the manufacturers, taking your discounts—"

"You're telling me! It would take two thousand pounds in hard cash to start that line, so let's pretend!"

"I could put two thousand pounds into the business, if you like."

"Good lord!" He was reproaching himself for having missed an opportunity. "Why should you? You don't like me any more."

"If you really mean that you could use the money, I'll see what a lawyer can do to help us."

The lawyer converted the business of J. Eshelby into a limited company with a capital of three thousand & 1 shares, of which two-thirds were owned by Mrs. Eshelby—whose signature would hence-forth be required on all checks drawn on the company's account. Pending dividends, each would draw a small salary from the company.

Eshelby made no comment about the articles of the company until the end of the day.

"Means you're boss of the show now, and can kick me out whenever you feel like it," he pointed out. "Not that that makes any change either of us'll notice."

"Did you want the money as a free gift?" countered Margaret. "Oh, don't be bitter and silly, Jim! It'll be fun, if you look at it in the right way. Let's go out and have a special dinner to celebrate."

"That's an *idea!*" he cried. "A better dinner than all the other dinners put together! Where'll you have yours? I'm going to have mine at the *Red Lion*—in the saloon for men only. See you later!"

Margaret watched him go without protest. It was the first time he had been out alone in the evening. His fear of her was weakening.

Within two hours he came home. His step on the stairs was not quite steady. He did not join her in the sitting room, but went to his own room and locked the door.

At breakfast he was in good spirits.

"Sorry about last night—I didn't mean it."

"I know you didn't mean it, Jim." When he smiled, she added, "That's why it's so discouraging. You give way to momentary impulses and are sorry for it afterwards. You don't remember how dangerous it is."

"A great deal in what you say!" he muttered. He was not really paying attention. He did not care whether she forgave him or not. His mind was occupied with the day's work, of which he began to talk excitedly.

When the office was closed for the lunch hour she went out and bought a bottle of whisky, which cost nearly two pounds. Men of his kind, she knew, very rarely kept alcoholic drinks in the home. He thought it a good idea and bought the next, and subsequent bottles, himself. He would drink quite heavily in the evenings—without, apparently, any loss of energy and enthusiasm during the day.

His enthusiasm mystified her. Apparently she had changed his views about the limited company. The use of her capital nearly doubled the former profits. This fired his imagination, and he drove himself hard, taking full advantage of a mild boom in the trade to secure new business.

"It's piling up and up and *up!*" he chirped. "What about declaring a dividend just for our two selves? I'm getting a bit short."

"We can't draw against profits until they're correctly declared," she told him, having been well coached by her lawyer. "The accounts have to be audited. But you can have an advance on your salary."

"I don't mind what they call it as long as it's cash!" He signed for an advance. He asked for another advance in a fortnight, and Margaret made no objection. The empty whisky bottles accumulated.

As month followed month he continued to work industriously and to enjoy it. In this, the third phase of their marriage, he seemed to have solved the problem of "treatment" by applying it to himself without her aid. He was regular in his habits, energetic and prudent in his work, and noticeably self-controlled. He would take small reverses and disappointments without even a swear word. In the office he left nothing to be desired. In the home he would speak politely, but he avoided her when he could. She knew why. He had turned her into the wife in his original nightmare of marriage. She remembered his words—"coming home every evening to the same woman and seeing her first thing every morning"—but she forgot that this was the reason he gave for murdering Eileen.

In due course the audit showed a net profit of close to a thousand pounds for the first half year. The formal meeting of the Board was held in Eshelby's office, under the wing of Margaret's lawyer. Eshelby did not listen carefully to the proceedings. He heard Margaret talking about the company acquiring a warehouse of its own, as the present structure in the backyard was inconvenient and otherwise inadequate to their expanding business. Eshelby assumed she was talking big to impress the lawyer's clerks.

"A thousand in the clear the first six months, and more to come! I told you it was piling up, didn't I?" The meeting was over, and Eshelby felt entitled to jubilate. "If I've got it right, that's around six hundred for you and three for me. A hundred'll do me to be going on with."

"But Jim! You heard what was said. The profits are ploughed back for development. You voted for it yourself. There is no dividend."

He was too alarmed for speech. He stared at her, his jaw loose.

"And the auditor says the advances made to you must be repaid by agreed deductions from your salary."

That finished it! She had taken his business away from him, and had now found another legal trick for making him work for nothing but his keep. What was the good of his keep if he had to share it with her? Sit opposite her or trot beside her to a film, wishing she was dead.

Enslaved for life.

Margaret was observing him. He was hunched in his chair, looking the way he had looked that first day when he was waiting for her to summon the police. A more virile man, she thought, would have stormed and brawled. Possibly her measures had been too drastic. She would ease things a little for him—provided he would cooperate. Say, pocket money. And perhaps a television set.

His limpness continued for the rest of the day. In the evening he barely touched his food. He was silent, answering absently when she spoke. When he went to bed, he took the whisky bottle with him. She had small jobs which busied her for an hour before she also retired.

She was in her dressing gown, brushing her hair, when she heard his footstep in the corridor. In his house, she had always left her door unlocked—"on principle." She could rush and lock it now. Instead, she went on brushing her hair.

He came in without knocking. She saw in the mirror that he had changed his lounge suit for an old pullover and flannel trousers.

"Well, Jim?"

"I've figured it out." The deep voice was husky. He closed the door, came slowly towards her. She was alert but not afraid, convinced that she could dominate him. He had been drinking, but he was by no means drunk.

Their eyes met in the looking glass. His were bloodshot, but fully perceptive.

"D'you know what you're doing, Margaret? . . . Murder!"

His voice had risen in pitch. The words were meaningless, she thought—which might be a bad sign. She kept her eyes fixed on his reflection. She knew he was quick and strong. But she would not have to scuffle—only to jerk him back to his senses.

"If you want to talk about the Board meeting, which you never trouble to understand—"

"I understand *you*, anyway—and I know where I get off." He spoke without anger, as if stating an impersonal opinion, and continued in the same detached tone. "I was a fool to choose you instead of the cops. I don't blame you for that."

"What *do* you blame me for, Jim?"

"Murder. Malice aforethought an' all!" He seemed to lose interest in her; he began to pace the room. "I was fond of Eileen. Lost my temper and found I'd done the poor kid in. You didn't lose *your* temper. Took it easy, you did—how long've we been married? Married—cor! I knew it wouldn't work. I've been living on borrowed time."

The old pullover and flannels began to take on meaning—she

had been told that suicides often take pains to avoid spoiling their clothes. Well, of course, she could jerk him out of that mood as easily as she could have jerked him out of the other.

"Figure it out, Margaret." He spoke from the doorway. Presently she heard him going downstairs. She felt certain that if she were to call him he would stop. She could exhibit concern, promise substantial concessions—

*(In those rare cases where treatment proved of no avail, the final outrage could be avoided if the patient were allowed to extinguish himself.)*

She heard the front door bang. She shielded her eyes with the curtain and looked out of the window. She looked left towards the main road—then right, which led nowhere except to the river. As once before, she looked for "the brand of Cain"—this time in her looking glass. Dismissing the childish fancy, she let her eyes rest on herself, with some complacency. Peach nylons and lace! She had always been ready to do everything she could to please him, in every way ...

He did not appear at breakfast. She ascertained that his bed had not been slept in then told herself that he had broken the rules. At the usual time she started work in the office, stopped in the middle of a letter and went to the storehouse in the yard. When she found him hanging from the centre beam she felt neither surprise nor horror. She was aware only of defeat.

# Chapter Six

By two o'clock, the body had been removed and the first stage in the coroner's routine had been completed. She shut the office for the day and took a taxi to Scotland Yard where she gave her married name and asked for Inspector Curwen.

She had to explain her business so she said she wished to make a statement about her husband's suicide. This had not yet been reported and there was some confusion and repetition before she was shown into Inspector Curwen's room.

"Good afternoon, Mrs. Eshelby. Why, it's Miss Whinley—"

"I was, Inspector. Fancy your remembering!"

The banalities were breaking her line of thought, blurring her sense of direction.

"We met at your flat. About the murder of your friend, Eileen Rivers." The Inspector was being jolly about it. "Your husband has hanged himself, I understand? Will you sit here? If you tell me anything I must ask questions."

"Then I'll answer the worst questions before you ask them," offered Margaret. "Our marriage was an unhappy one. Last night my husband said, in effect, that he intended to take his life. I more or less believed him. I think I could have persuaded him not to. But I did nothing."

"That's not a matter for the police." Curwen was remembering his own conclusions about this woman's disappearance. "What was your husband's occupation, Mrs. Eshelby?"

"A middleman. In sanitary fittings."

Sanitary fittings! That made Curwen virtually certain.

"When were you married, Mrs. Eshelby?"

"Last year. July the twenty-seventh."

"That would be about five weeks after he had murdered your friend, wouldn't it?"

"Yes," answered Margaret, throwing Curwen off his balance. He did not want a confession from her. He had proof from the dead girl's diary that Margaret had not met 'Grantham' before the murder. At worst, she was a compassionate accessory—a charge which was rarely worth making.

"Did your husband confess to you that he had murdered your friend?"

"Of course! That was why I married him."

Curwen stroked the back of his head. An odd bird, this woman, but that was her affair. He drew from her all the details of the murder which Eshelby had given her.

"Didn't you realize, Mrs. Eshelby, that it was your duty to report to us?"

"It was a matter of principle," she answered. "I have always believed it wrong to hang anybody. So I had to accept responsibility for him. I made a mess of the job."

"So you married him—" Curwen noted that she was not unattractive physically—"to reform him. And if he wouldn't reform, there was always us at the end of a telephone!"

"I suppose it was a sort of blackmail," conceded Margaret. "But for a moral purpose, of course. I wanted to force him into a way of living which would turn him into a good citizen—"

"*Like you?*"

Margaret could not be certain that the Inspector had spoken the words. A truth had struck her a glancing blow. She groped back to her defense, but again she lost direction.

"My method was succeeding. He worked very hard, built up his business and—behaved himself. But I blundered by making the conditions so harsh that he broke down. He said it was I who was really the murderer. It's nonsense, but it does contain a grain of truth. That's why I have come here to be prosecuted for shielding a murderer."

"Then you've come to the wrong shop for what you want, Mrs.

Eshelby!" snapped Curwen. "Your conscience is no business of ours. I don't say you will not be prosecuted—that's for the higher authorities—but I shall be very surprised if we are ordered to take action. Thank you for answering my questions."

"But, Inspector—"

"Good afternoon, Mrs. Eshelby. Please let us know if you change your address."

Late that afternoon she observed that the coroner's man had not sealed the 'warehouse' though he had said he would do so.

She went in, wishing to recapture the mood in which he had killed himself. She felt a gentleness towards him that was akin to mourning. She travelled backwards in their shared history of which a part was her daydream of Eileen's lover before she had ever seen him. Perhaps the most important part.

Again she ran the gamut of horror in the presence of the murderer of her friend, the moment of daring in which she inverted the moral values of civilization, to the honeymoon and the early days of their marriage when she believed the daydream had been realized. Had she survived the humiliation of his rejection and honestly served the ideal which she had concocted from the pamphlets of her childhood? Or had her harshness been instructed by revenge?

"Figure it out, Margaret."

The beam, a slender looking steel rod, had not been bent by his weight. You made a noose at each end of the rope. You threaded one noose through the other round the beam. For that you would need the steps—over there, behind the self-flushes ... Then you greased the length of the rope ... This empty packing case was about the right height ...

*Spinster's Evidence*

# Chapter One

It has been noted before that murder by means of poison in a cocktail glass has a distorting effect on the public imagination—even the police will play parlor games with the glasses. In the Chermouth case there were three cocktail glasses, one loaded with the poison, on a small circular tray. Circular tray! Turn the tray by accident or design and the three glasses will produce eighteen theories. Still more theories can be pinned on the guess that the murderer, "adroitly diverting the attention of his victim," switches the glasses—which includes the intriguing possibility that he may be so muddled by the circularity of the tray that he bumps himself off!

There was no switching of glasses—no "adroitness" by anybody—in the Chermouth case. None of the stock theories fitted, because it was not a stock kind of murder.

It occurred at twenty-three past seven on a Monday evening in April. The time, like nearly every other relevant fact, was fixed by Miss Humby, an eye-witness who saved the police mountains of work.

Gladys Humby, though not thirty, was an active, dumpy little spinster, with an active, dumpy little mind. Clever people cannot predict what will interest a fool. No clever or intelligent person, completely unaware that a murder was in the course of being committed, would have observed all the small actions of everybody around her. But Miss Humby, being what she was, rarely observed anything else.

Chermouth, some twenty miles out of London, was hardly more than an overgrown village. The residents were social and informal and knew each other's affairs. Thus it was known that on most

Monday evenings during the winter, Miss Humby dined with the Esdales and Lyle Brocker, to make a fourth at bridge.

At a quarter to seven, she entered the front garden of The Bines. It was a prematurely warm evening and she was *so* pleased that the french windows of the sitting-room were open because it was a sign that summer had almost come. It was an early Victorian house. The young Esdales had removed the folding doors between the one-time dining and drawing-rooms, thereby making one long room. Miss Humby approached the windows.

"May I come in?" she called. "Or must I ring the bell like a perfect lady?"

A moment later she saw that the room contained only her fellow guest, Lyle Brocker. He was coming towards her from the dining-room end.

"Hullo, Gladys! Joan has just rushed upstairs—George knocked something over, I think. Give 'em a few minutes, then we'll organize a rescue party."

"I wonder what he knocked over, but I expect they'll tell us ... I see they've bought *River Yachting* too." It was one of those very large, flat books that are virtually albums, and it was lying on top of the radio console. "Oh, but it's your copy! Joan will spill things on it ... I must just take a peep at their primulas." She was moving towards the windows, of identical pattern, at the other end of the room. "Ours have been terribly disappointing."

Lyle Brocker never took any notice of her when she chattered and little enough at any other time. When they were in their late 'teens she had been a bit of a nuisance, but nowadays he felt only compassion for a girl who had lost her way in life.

Brocker, dark, large, but nimble, was a metallurgist, a coming man in the firm that employed him. To Miss Humby, he was a fairy prince, scaled down to marriageable proportions. She knew there were those who saw him as a wistful figure, deemed to be nursing a secret sorrow, in that he had once been engaged to Joan, whom he had known since they were children. That was three years ago. Miss Humby was sure it couldn't have meant much because, within a year, Joan had married George Esdale, a barrister who was already making his mark. She would not call George handsome, though he was kind—and very clever, people said.

A few minutes after Miss Humby's arrival, at exactly nine minutes to seven, Joan appeared, pattering over her shoulder to her husband, who presently joined her in the doorway.

"Sorry, Gladys. George felt he had to try his brute strength on the medicine cabinet, and smashed everything. By the way he bellowed, I thought he had hurt himself."

"I wasn't bellowing—I was only swearing. At you, dear, for shifting the thing without warning me."

Thus the evening began—and continued for the next twenty minutes—like any other evening, anywhere, when familiar friends gather to pass time. There were the same banalities, the same elaboration of trivial incidents, the slight fussing to promote sociability.

Miss Humby derived pleasure from the fact that Joan was wearing her violet semi-evening gown, of the same hue as her eyes. She thought that Joan was very lovely but that she was beginning to lose her looks, a bad sign at twenty-seven. She was certainly thinner than she used to be and there were times, of late, when she had looked nearly haggard. She had also observed that George Esdale and Lyle Brocker were both afflicted with stigmata of advancing years, though both were of the same age as herself. She did not allow herself to draw any inference from these observations.

The chatter was general until the two men slipped into politics. At two minutes to seven, Joan got up to mix the drinks and Miss Humby followed her into the dining-room half of the room—part of the ritual of every Monday evening.

On their left was the dining-table, laid and covered with muslin by the help, who left at five. Against the wall on their right was the sideboard, and between the two at the far end of the room, were the second pair of french windows giving on to the garden at the rear of the house. The sideboard, of the same period as the house, contained two cupboards, a table-board some five feet in length, and a bay for a spirit tantalus which rested between two smaller cupboards for cigars and liqueurs. Laid in readiness on the table-board were four coffee cups, a glass percolator, a bottle of gin, and a bottle of vermouth. The two bottles were about three-quarters full. Beside the two bottles was the small circular tray on which stood the three cocktail glasses.

When the two women approached the sideboard, one of the three glasses—it was contended—already contained the poison, in the form of approximately half a teaspoon of a liquid which is colorless and odorless. It was possible, therefore, that Joan was ignorant of the presence of the poison.

"Break the rule of a lifetime, Gladys, and have a drink," invited Joan.

"No, thank you, dear." Miss Humby meticulously adjusted the box of matches which was half out of its clip on the pedestal of the percolator. "I was persuaded to drink gin once and I felt awful afterwards. They say smoking—at least you two don't smoke!—smoking and drinking alcohol make you old before your time. I wonder you can take the dreadful stuff."

"I don't drink very much," said Joan. "Only half as much as I give the men—I fill up with vermouth."

She poured a small tot of gin into one of the glasses.

"There! Even that is a little more than I generally take."

She added vermouth, then filled the other two glasses.

"They all look the same," said Miss Humby. "How do you tell yours from the others?"

"Mine's the one nearest to me." Joan picked up the tray and Miss Humby noticed that Joan's thumb was nearest to the glass in which she had put the short tot of gin.

"It's getting chilly," remarked Joan. She raised her voice. "Geoorge! Shut the big windows, darling! We'll have the little ones open at each end. I'll do this one."

Joan put the circular tray back on the sideboard, then went to the window and opened the small panel in the larger pane. When she returned, the sideboard was on her left. She picked up the circular tray with her left hand, which was nearer.

There was a sharp draught between the panels at opposite ends of the long room. Miss Humby shivered elaborately—she lived in fear of draughts.

"I fancy George will want to cry off bridge next week," Joan said. "He likes to potter about with a trowel at the first sign of summer."

"Just what I was going to suggest, dear," said Miss Humby, noticing that Joan had changed the tray back to her right hand while she was speaking and that her thumb was not nearer one glass than another.

Lyle Brocker was sitting in the armchair near the window. George was wandering about the room. Lyle got up as Joan approached. He took a glass from the tray, then sank back into the armchair.

Joan always sat in a corner of the settee. As George was still wandering, she put a glass for herself on the radio cabinet, within arm's reach of the settee. Actually, she put the glass on top of Lyle Brocker's copy of *River Yachting*. Then she crossed the room and placed the tray—on which there was now only one glass—on the bookcase, for her husband.

While Joan was at the bookcase Miss Humby removed *River Yachting* from under the cocktail glass and pointedly put the book on Lyle's knee. Then, after noting that she and Joan had taken four minutes while mixing the drinks, she sat beside Joan on the settee.

George, after shutting the panel at the far end of the room, came back, in the direction of the bookcase.

Suddenly, Miss Humby thought of something.

"Joan! You didn't keep track of your glass," she said. "You changed hands twice."

"*Did* she!" exclaimed George. "If I've got hers, I'm entitled to another to keep pace with Lyle. We'll soon see!"

George took the glass from the tray on the bookcase and drank the whole of the contents. This mild clowning amused Miss Humby. Later, of course, it became extremely important evidence. It raised the question: If George had known that one of the glasses contained poison, would he not have waited, before drinking, until the first symptom of poisoning appeared in his victim?

"That seemed strong enough," he said, and glanced at Lyle, who was talking to Joan. Lyle's glass remained untouched on the occasional table. It was now five minutes past seven.

"I may as well tell you, Gladys," said George, "that you're getting the same meal as you had last Monday. The difference is that it's my turn to heat up the soup. How do you like your soup heated?"

"If you're nervous about it, I'll come and help you," tittered Miss Humby.

"No, thank you. You can help by seeing that they don't take too long over their drinks. I know the soup oughtn't to boil."

Joan, Miss Humby happened to know, always made soup from stock, so there would be no tins to be opened. It would take about four minutes to heat enough soup for four. Six minutes past seven. She checked the clock by her wrist-watch which had been checked an hour ago by radio. Six past seven on the dot. Silly of George to tell her to hurry the others over their drinks. How could she?

Besides, Joan had already taken two sips and was keeping the glass in her hand. Lyle had taken up his glass but had put it down again untouched while he explained to Joan something about the river rising on the spring tide. They were both looking solemnly at each other as if it were frightfully important, which it couldn't possibly be.

At twelve minutes past seven, Joan glanced at the clock, then took quite a big sip. She swirled the liquid as if she thought it hadn't mixed properly, then took another big sip which left her glass practically empty. She put the glass back on the radio.

"You are wrong in supposing that the wind can have little or no effect on the flood tide." They might almost have been quarrelling about it. And then—strangely enough thought Miss Humby—Lyle picked up his glass and again put it down without drinking, because he seemed so worked up about the wind and the tide.

Joan touched Miss Humby's arm.

"It's getting frightfully hot in here. I think we'd better have the big windows open again."

"I'll do it," said Lyle. As he rose, he took up his glass, drank half the contents, and then continued talking, while he opened the french windows: "The north wind piles up the seas in the bottleneck of Dover and Calais—"

"I'm boiling hot," cried Joan. "There must be something wrong with that vermouth—don't drink it, Lyle!"

"There can't be—mine tasted all right." The next moment he was at her side, holding her in his arms.

"Joan, darling, what is the matter with you?"

"I can't breathe—I must have air—I'm frightfully ill!"

He laid her full length on the settee. He shouted for George, then rushed out through the windows for Dr. Blagrove, knowing it would be quicker than telephoning.

It was exactly twenty-two minutes past seven.

"Gladys!"

"Yes, darling. Dr. Blagrove will be here in a minute . . . Hold on to me if it helps."

"Gladys, listen to me!"

The physical circumstances of the next thirty seconds are unimportant. Speech was blurred and irregular, but Miss Humby was able to hear and later to report as if the words had been uttered continuously. The words were repetitive. Soon they ceased altogether.

Presently, Miss Humby became aware that George had come into the room and that he was supporting her to a chair. She was crying but was able to observe George, who exhibited nothing but bewilderment.

"George! Did you hear what she said?"

"No. When I came in she was—like that."

"She said she had put poison in her drink. She said she meant to kill herself. She kept repeating it."

"It may be true," said George.

Dr. Blagrove came in through the french windows, followed by Lyle Brocker. George looked past Blagrove as if he were not present and spoke to Lyle.

"Joan told Gladys she put poison in her glass because she wanted to kill herself."

"I thought of that while I was fetching Blagrove," said Lyle. "I wonder . . ."

# Chapter Two

Within forty minutes of Joan Esdale's death, Colonel Maenmore, the Chief Constable of the county, arrived and received Inspector Rouse's report, covering routine.

"The three glasses were identified unanimously by the three survivors. There was enough left in each for analysis, but Dr. Blagrove says that, from the symptoms, he's certain it was—eczymo-something—it's here in the medical report, sir."

"That means plenty of leg work for your men." Maenmore had read the report. "Worse than weed-killer or fly papers to trace. What do they call the commercial stuff?—Kilfly. Three-ounce bottles in every chemist's and oilshop in the country. From half a gallon of it, anybody can distil a fatal dose—as little as five drops."

"Yes, sir. I've asked the three of 'em to wait in a bedroom upstairs." They were speaking in the morning-room, on the opposite side of the corridor, which George Esdale had offered. "They're all fully co-operative." He lowered his voice: "You might like to see that Miss Humby first, sir. She's very useful—the Nosey Parker miss."

"Put her in this room, while I have a look round."

The technical men had nearly finished. He gave permission for the body to be taken to the mortuary.

Maenmore had the physique of a retired army officer, with the face of an amiable scholar. Though he had served successfully for ten years in the military police, the civil force regarded him as something of an armchair amateur—a belief which Maenmore himself encouraged.

In a couple of minutes he realized that Miss Humby was a

policeman's dream come true. He cut his questions and invited her to give him a full account of everything, beginning with her own arrival at the house. Miss Humby took him at his word. The result was the next best thing to a talking film of the whole incident.

From Brocker, whom he saw next, he received a report which dovetailed with that of Miss Humby.

"When Miss Humby arrived, you were alone in the room. Where were you actually sitting?"

"I was at the dining-room end, at the sideboard, when I heard her voice in the garden. I had run short of matches and I knew they kept the only box of matches in the house on a little clip in the coffee percolator, which works on a spirit lamp."

"An unfortunate spot, in the circumstances," remarked Maenmore. "Why is it the only box in the house?"

"They have an electric cooker and they don't smoke," said Brocker, patiently. "Esdale does jury work and he's as careful about his voice as a singer."

"So you went to the sideboard, lit a cigarette—"

"I smoke a pipe—that's why I don't carry a lighter. I took half the contents of the match-box and put them in my own empty box—I know the Esdales very well."

"You were heard to express the opinion that deceased had committed suicide, Mr. Brocker?"

"I admit that was my idea, at first." Brocker stroked his chin. "But I can't see how she worked it. She did not put anything in her glass after she came along with the tray. Besides, if she intended to commit suicide she wouldn't do it in such a way that she might kill somebody else instead. As it was, any one of us might have swallowed that poison—except Miss Humby."

Maenmore was holding his fire. It would be idle to ask Brocker why he had not touched his drink until Mrs. Esdale had revealed the first symptom of poisoning—alternatively, why he did not believe her when she warned him that there was "something wrong with that vermouth."

Before sending for Esdale, Maenmore went to the sideboard in the main room. The bottles had been removed for analysis, but the coffee outfit was untouched. Fitted to the supporting column of the percolator was a clip for holding the standard-size box of safety matches.

There was no box of matches in the clip.

Brocker had stated specifically that he had taken half the matches from the box, implying that he had left the box itself still there. That, Maenmore reflected, was the sort of irritating trifle that so often caused a lot of work for nothing.

Now for the husband . . .

The principle that, when a wife has been murdered, the husband is the first suspect could hardly be applied. The husband had been the first to drink—and he had drained his glass at a gulp.

When George Esdale presented himself, Maenmore spoke gently, as to a stricken man, while taking him over the now familiar ground. He soon perceived that restraint would be unnecessary. The deceased woman was not lamented. Miss Humby, her intimate friend, had shown only a reporter's concern. Brocker had been convincing as an interested spectator. The husband was taking his wife's death as a problem of human conduct.

"So, as soon as the drinks had been handed round you finished yours quickly and left the room. Will you tell me exactly what you did between then and the moment when you re-entered the sitting-room?"

"I went from the sitting-room to the kitchen and put on a saucepan of soup to heat. I stayed there until Brocker shouted."

"But you did not come at once?"

"Almost at once. At first I was not certain I had heard the shout. A little later I came to the conclusion that it must have been a shout and that it was my name."

"I'd like to get these small things buttoned up," said Maenmore. "If you don't mind, we'll check on that shout. Shall we go to the kitchen?"

Maenmore told Rouse to ask Brocker to co-operate. When Esdale opened the door of the kitchen there was an unpleasant smell, not a little smoke, and a mess on the electric cooker. The soup had boiled over; what was left had evaporated and the bottom of the saucepan was red-hot.

"Good Lord, I forgot all about it!" Esdale turned the switch. Maenmore shut the kitchen door. Presently from the sitting-room Brocker's voice was most distinctly heard calling, "George."

"That's unmistakable," said Esdale. "I suppose I was wool-gathering."

Back in the morning-room, Maenmore elicited that it was George Esdale who had taken the bottles of vermouth and gin and the three glasses from the cupboard, as soon as he arrived home.

"When the glasses were in the cupboard," asked Maenmore, "were they right side up?"

"No. Upside down—I suppose to keep the dust out."

That eliminated the daily help and prepared the way for the pivotal question.

"Mr. Esdale, do you believe your wife committed suicide?"

"I can't make up my mind. Apparently she said so—and when Miss Humby told me, I thought it might be true. Since then, I've been wondering whether Miss Humby might possibly have misunderstood what my wife did say."

"Miss Humby was very definite."

"She always is," smiled Esdale. "She was also definite in explaining how my wife had done this and that with the tray, so there was no telling one glass from another. That doesn't marry up with the statement that Joan knew one of the glasses contained poison."

The Chief Constable reminded himself that this man was a lawyer and would know the rules of evidence. Even so, he had misstated the facts.

"Miss Humby reports only the fact that your wife *said* she poisoned herself. Her statement to Miss Humby may have been a gallant lie. She realized that she had been poisoned. Assume that she suspected the poisoner was a man she loved and that she wished to forego vengeance. Women have behaved like that before."

"Y-yes. That's a feasible theory of what might have been in her mind. She assumed I had poisoned her."

"Had she any reason for such a suspicion?"

"She had as much and as little reason as I have to suspect that it was she who tried to poison me. You realize, Colonel, that there's just as strong and just as weak a case that way round?"

There was a long silence.

"Keep going, Mr. Esdale. I've been waiting for you to mention Brocker as potential murderer. It'll work 'that way round' too, won't it?"

"You can nominate Brocker. And I can suggest Miss Humby. You seem to want my view of the case. Here it is. That poison got into that glass by blind chance, or it was put in by one of the *four* of us for the purpose of suicide or murder. Take any one of us as the hypothetical murderer and you get absurdity. Miss Humby issues a public warning that the glasses have been mixed up. What is the hypothetical murderer's next move? Obviously to prevent the other two from drinking—no matter how! Anything would be preferable to the risk of being accused of murdering the wrong person. But the hypothetical murderer made no move at all. He—or she—sits like a ninny saying, 'Bless my soul! The wrong person may be killed. There's one chance in three it will be so, so I won't touch my glass until somebody else starts dying.' It just couldn't happen like that!"

But part of it had happened like that. In sketching an absurdity, Esdale had described what Brocker had actually done.

"Murderers rarely behave consistently. Ignoring reasonableness of behavior, can you suggest any motive?"

"Ignoring reasonableness of behavior," echoed Esdale, "I can supply motives for two. My wife and myself. Our marriage was not a success. There was no cat-and-dog element. But—in a subtle sort of way—we stood in each other's light."

In a dozen sentences George Esdale gave the history of his marriage—truthful, as far as it went. But there are some things which not even a policeman expects a man to say about his wife . . .

If Joan Barnaby had been predatory, shallow, and cruel, she would probably have done little harm to anybody. By a simple paradox, it was her ingrained honesty, her kindliness and integrity, that made her father's home life thoroughly uncomfortable, that frustrated a handful of admirers and completely wrecked her very promising marriage.

She was possessed of a vital turbulence which would infect others when she was herself disturbed, though men not attuned to her saw only a good-looking girl who could be very lively when she chose. She had a lithe body, of irreproachable outline, dark hair, near-violet eyes, and a profile that made photographers think well of themselves.

Her mother died when Joan was five, leaving the child an income sufficient—as Joan discovered before she was twelve—to pay her boarding-school fees.

At the time of Mrs. Barnaby's death, Gladys Humby elected herself Big Sister to give solace and practical guidance. Joan never forgot her debt of friendship, though as adults she and Gladys had little in common.

At eighteen, Joan went up to Cambridge. At twenty, she joined a repertory company as an amateur. She had a small talent, but lacked the passionate desire for a career. For three years, she worked and idled at various arts, crafts, and sports until the day when Gladys Humby made an extremely personal confidence. It was all very arch and indefinite, but the upshot was that Gladys was deeply interested in Lyle Brocker, with whom Joan was on tomboyish, cousinly terms. Joan made the right answers, while inwardly she felt only pity for poor Gladys, who was already a predestined spinster but didn't know it.

Ten days later, Joan made the sudden discovery that she herself had been in love with Lyle Brocker all her life. She was unaware of the magnetic nature of her own disturbances and therefore honestly believed it to be sheer coincidence when he proposed to her at their next meeting.

Her engagement to Lyle, announced in April, was warmly approved by her father and by all concerned—with the negligible exception of Gladys Humby, whose reactions Joan failed to consider important.

The engagement lasted six weeks, then foundered on an episode involving Lyle Brocker and a red-headed beauty employed as a secretary in his firm. Shortly afterwards, Lyle was transferred, at his own request, to the Amsterdam branch.

Joan did not seem to suffer. She stated what she honestly believed to be her position when her father ventured to console her.

"There's nothing in it, Daddy. People change, and I'm one of those who change with a bang instead of gradually. It isn't a 'knock' for me, as you seem to think."

It had been a knock for Captain Barnaby. His affection for his daughter did not obscure the truth that she was self-centered, even though she was not selfish. She was egotistical, even though she was not conceited. A husband, he thought, would manage that sort of thing much better than a father.

George Esdale lived in London, but in Chermouth he had a resident aunt who made herself useful. It was again April when Esdale felt he had waited long enough.

"I will not press you for an answer to this question." It was the kind of thing he said in court, so it made him feel safe. "Have you forgotten Brocker?"

"Yes—except as an event. It was the afterglow of a childish adoration. I don't regret it—it made me realize that part of me was a sentimental fake. I changed—with a bang—and became myself."

George and Joan were married in June, Gladys Humby being chief bridesmaid. Joan's father—for the second time warmly approving his daughter's engagement—presented them with his house and went to live with his widowed sister in Hampstead.

Joan didn't "adore" George Esdale, but she loved him and enjoyed his companionship, which was richer than that of Lyle Brocker, and more understanding. They were wholly happy for two years.

Then, a few days after their second anniversary, Joan mentioned to George: "I've just heard that Lyle—Lyle Brocker, of course!—has been transferred back to London. He'll be living with his people, as he did before. It's that Georgian house up the road, with the big cedars. There's no need for any of us to be self-conscious, is there?"

"I've no feeling about it, if you haven't."

"I've none at all. And I'd hate to be stand-offish with Lyle—I still call his father 'Uncle Arthur.'"

A week later, Joan and Lyle met and greeted each other boisterously, which was natural enough since they had been honorary cousins from childhood. The Esdales went to dinner with the Brockers, father and son. No one was ill at ease about anything.

Often, Lyle and George would meet on the train, or give each other a lift. They discovered common interests. A friend of Brocker's had a small yacht, and the Esdales would make up a party of four, sailing on the Thames. George persuaded Lyle to take up golf seriously.

One night in October, when Lyle Brocker came to dinner, Gladys Humby, their fourth at bridge, failed them at the last minute. After dinner, George Esdale was called to the telephone and was absent for about ten minutes. Shortly afterwards Lyle took a rather abrupt departure.

"Washout!" exclaimed George. "Gladys has killed the evening. Break her neck, darling, next time you see her."

Joan, bolt upright on the settee, looked at him absently, not knowing what he had said.

"The money Mother left me!" she exclaimed. "George, I want us to give this house back to Daddy and use my money to buy another—anywhere you like."

That was enough to tell George most of it. But he had to make sure.

"Lyle?" he asked.

"Yes."

"But you said you had no feeling in that direction?" It was a puzzled question, without reproach. "Have you—changed back?"

"With a bang!" She smiled, but she was crying, silently. "There was no feeling—until tonight—until you went to that damned telephone and left us alone!"

She was crying quite a lot but still making no sound with it. He could not comfort her until he had shuffled his own thoughts. He grasped immediately that their future hung upon his behavior in the next few minutes.

"Would you care to tell me exactly what happened?"

"I'll try. But there's no *incident*, George! He didn't move from his chair—and I was sitting here all the time. We didn't speak, in the beginning. I began to feel he was looking at me and I tried not to look at him. I think we were looking at each other a long time—a very long time. And then he said, 'We've torn it this time, Joan.' It was the way he said it. And then you came in. It certainly wasn't his fault. I suppose it's mine, though I can't quite see how."

George knew her well enough to be confident that she was not fooling herself. There was the bare hope that it might be no more than the welling up of childish memories in a sudden hysteria.

"I don't think"—he was weighing his words, "I don't think it's a good idea to run away."

"George! You don't *want* me to see him again, after what I've told you?"

"If Lyle were to vanish from the earth, I'd be delighted. But he exists. He's not an enemy—he's a problem. It's a delusion to believe that you can run away from him. We might never again see his face—but he'd be living with us all the same."

"Don't!" She covered her eyes with her hands. Her distress shook him a little, revealed that there was more danger of losing her than he had thought. But he could not hold her by reminding her of her marriage vows, since she had obviously not forgotten them.

"Assuming that you are right about his feelings and equally right about your own, would you like a divorce?"

"No!" That was very definite. "I would tell you if I did. I just want—oh, to forget that it flared up! You must help me, George—you must!"

"If we run away I can't help you, however hard I try. The dream-lover sheds all human weaknesses. No husband can possibly compete with him."

"Then, must we go on as we are?"

"It's the safest course for all three of us. A commonplace everyday atmosphere may save us. Take another look at Lyle—in his unromantic moods. Let him take another look at you, ditto."

That did not please her.

"Do you mean that you hope I shall fall *out* of love with him?"

"Or out of love with me. Helping me to be glad to let you go." Before she could object, he went on: "You love him enough to be frightened of your own reactions. And you love me enough to want to preserve our marriage. That's a deadlock which no single one of us can break."

"So we'll all three break it together—or give it a chance to break itself!" She was adopting the idea all too eagerly. "You're being wonderful about it, George dear!"

Her arms were outstretched. Gently, he held her off.

"I think we must wait," he said, "until we've—all three—made up our minds."

# Chapter Three

Lyle Brocker was also alarmed. There had been an "interlude" in Amsterdam which had encouraged him to believe he had emotionally forgotten Joan. He had believed it right up to the moment when the disturbance in herself had drawn his eyes to hers and reawakened him.

He would have to clear out and not see Joan again.

But before he could say anything about moving, she announced: "I told George! He thinks we oughtn't to make a crisis of it but carry on as we are and give it a fair chance to blow over."

"Blow over!" Lyle made a noise like laughter. "Or blow up! Let me tell you that you were a fool to throw us away over that girl you called 'red-head.'"

"And a cad for loving George—which I do! He offered a divorce, but I didn't accept. It would be no use, because I would always be remembering how vilely I had treated him. And that would bore you—and I should fall between two stools."

"You can't have two stools. You oughtn't even to think like that. I wish I could despise you for it—and be free. And then we could be three jolly good friends again."

The attempt to laugh at themselves was a failure, but after a month or so it looked as if the plan as a whole might succeed. Among other devices, the Monday evenings of bridge were started. Gladys Humby, roped in as a permanent fourth, began by misinterpreting Lyle Brocker's courtesy in escorting her home—thereby plunging herself into the emotional whirlpool.

At first, there was some self-consciousness in the three principals, expressed in excessive heartiness. This passed into an intermediate phase in which deep feeling seemed to be suspended. It was an illusion produced by mutual tolerance and good manners—refinements of civilized man to which the nervous system has not yet adjusted itself.

In time, Gladys perceived that being escorted home by Lyle was, in itself, profitless. She would lie awake assuring herself that Joan could not possibly be running Lyle on a string simply to prevent another woman from monopolizing him.

By the turn of the year it was tacitly accepted that the plan had failed. Lyle told Joan that it would be better for him to leave Chermouth as originally intended. Joan said it would be unnecessary since she herself had thought of going to stay with a relative in Scotland for six months. When she told George, he said in that case he would look for rooms in London.

But none of them did anything about it, because the vicious circle had already closed.

The tolerance and the good manners, sustained in the presence of others, began slowly to wilt. There were triangular bickerings. The jungle was creeping in on them.

In her diary, Joan recorded her awareness that she was sinking in a quagmire of emotionalism. She realized with self-contempt that she had reached a state in which the power to make a decision had been lost. In this state she no longer felt any love for either George or Lyle, yet lacked the ability to run away from them.

At times, she wished one of them would die—she didn't care which; at other times she wished they would both be killed in a railway accident—anything to break out of the vicious circle.

She did not guess that George might have come to feeling about her as she felt about him—still less that Lyle would go to any length to tear her out of his imagination.

She allowed herself to be amused by Gladys Humby's futile hopes of Lyle Brocker.

"Looks as if we've got something here, sir," said Inspector Rouse. In his open hand was a phial, little more than an inch long. It was empty, but the cork had been replaced. "No prints—they've been wiped off. Found in the shrubbery of the front garden, ten feet from the windows."

The Chief Constable expressed approval, on principal. There could be little hope of tracing the phial itself. Moreover, it might have been flung into the garden of necessity, or placed there by design.

Presently, they went to the kitchen. The three witnesses were waiting "by request" at police headquarters, while the house was searched.

"Nothing in here, sir. The cooker is a super—quart of water boiled in five minutes."

Except for the mess made by the overboiling soup, the kitchen was excellently clean. Under the sink, upturned and glistening, was a garbage pail, beside it a half-burnt match. Maenmore removed the pail and found a second match, also half-burnt.

"Maybe the 'help' smokes," suggested Rouse, "though I can't see a hired woman throwing matches under the sink."

Maenmore looked under the sink at the curving waste-pipe.

"Have that swansneck opened, Inspector. And tell your men to find the box of matches that was clipped to the coffee percolator. It's less than half full and the box should bear the marks of the clip."

"Very good, sir!" Rouse suppressed a chuckle. This was the armchair touch. Lucky there was no cigarette ash to analyze.

In the study, next to the morning-room, the search party had created some confusion, which they would presently clear up. Maenmore was turning away when his eye was caught by a pamphlet which he recognized as the annual Report on the Metropolitan Police, recording the activities of Scotland Yard during the previous year. On the back cover of the pamphlet, which was blank, there was a column of figures in pencil. He contemplated the figures, then pocketed the pamphlet thoughtfully.

Upstairs, there was no difficulty in telling which of the four bedrooms had been Mrs. Esdale's. A strong breeze blew in his face as he opened the door. He looked round, receiving an impression of fastidiousness, though the room was surprisingly untidy. When he observed that the dressing-table had been pulled askew, the untidiness explained itself.

In a few minutes he found Mrs. Esdale's diary, to which he gave profound attention. He learned nothing about the manner of her death, but a great deal about her mentality. Incidentally, he received a picture of Miss Humby's character—with special reference to her emotional cross-currents—which came near to shocking him.

# Chapter Four

It was close on midnight when Miss Humby and the two men were invited from the waiting-room at county headquarters to Chief Constable Maenmore's office.

"Police procedure is designed for dealing with the criminal classes," the Colonel began. "You are not of the criminal classes—but one of you has committed murder. I shall expect the other two to assist me in completing my case against the guilty party."

"I will," murmured Miss Humby. She had tucked her feet under her chair, increasing the effect of dumpiness. At a separate table, Inspector Rouse was occupied with his official bag, which excited her curiosity.

"The poison could have been dropped into the glass before the three glasses were filled, at the sideboard, by the deceased. Each of you, including the deceased, had the opportunity to do so. In the reports which you have given me of your own and each other's movements, one item, however, is unaccounted for—the box of matches that was in the clip on the pedestal of the coffee percolator. Mr. Brocker, you told me you took some matches from the box. Are you quite sure you did not take the box itself?"

"He couldn't have," cut in Miss Humby. "I straightened that box while poor Joan was pouring the drinks. If it really matters what happened to a box of matches, the only person who could have taken it would be you, George, when you went to shut the panel in the window just before you had your drink, if you remember."

"I don't smoke. I never carry matches," said Esdale.

"We have searched the house and the garden for that box of

matches," Maenmore went on. "Mr. Esdale, will you please search your pockets?"

Esdale stood up, slapped his side pockets.

"Good heavens!" He laid a partly filled box of matches on the desk. "I'm very sorry, Colonel. I have no recollection whatever of picking it up. And I don't know whether it came from the percolator or not."

"There were no other boxes in your house." Maenmore passed the match-box to the Inspector. There was a long silence, while the latter opened his bag, took out a lens, and examined the match-box. He pressed carbon paper on the match-box and measured the result.

"This box," he announced, "has been held in a clip identical with the clip on that percolator."

From his pocket case, the Chief Constable shook out a fragment of stiff paper, folded. It was roughly triangular in shape and barely an inch at its greatest length.

"Will you look at that, Mr. Esdale, and tell me what it is?"

"I don't know what it is, but it looks like the corner of a correspondence envelope."

"It is just that," said Maenmore. "We found it in the waste-pipe of the sink in your kitchen, together with some ashes."

"Really?" Esdale was politely curious. "Does that lead to something?"

"You left the room, after gulping your drink, at six past seven." Maenmore glanced at Miss Humby, who murmured agreement. "But you did not go straight to the cooker and heat the soup. If you had done so it would have boiled over long before you left the kitchen, at, say, seven twenty-three. You went to your wife's bedroom. Your purpose was to retrieve a document which you had placed on her dressing-table. It was no longer there. After a somewhat frantic search you realized that it might have been blown from the dressing-table by the draught from the open window. You moved the dressing-table, found the document, then went to the kitchen and burned it over the sink. You then burned the envelope, using a total of two matches, which you threw under the sink. You bungled slightly with the envelope, burned your fingers, and dropped this fragment onto the wet sink. Being wet, it did not burn, so you flushed it down the waste-pipe of the sink. You had not quite finished all this when Mr. Brocker shouted. You were close-pressed for time, but you remembered to switch on the cooker under the saucepan."

"Amazing!" exclaimed Esdale. "But how does this fantasy link up with the death of my wife?"

"Oh, the link! Yes, of course." Maenmore produced from his breast pocket the annual Report on the activities of Scotland Yard. He turned the pamphlet to the blank back cover and pointed to the pencilled figures.

"I happen to have studied murder statistics too, Mr. Esdale, so I recognized some of the figures. The first figure is the total number of murders committed last year. The next three are deductions of murders believed to have been committed by perverts, maniacs, and professional criminals. The next to the last figure is the number of murders planned by non-criminals. The last figure shows that the chance of the latter escaping conviction is only one in nine-and-a-fraction."

"Quite right," agreed Esdale. "I remember working it out. It's nine to one that the premeditating murderer gets caught. I read a paper on that at the club last February."

"I can confirm that," said Brocker. "I was his guest at the club."

"Aren't we getting rather lost?" suggested Esdale. "You were going to tell us how all this links up with my wife's death, Colonel?"

"Did you know your wife kept a diary?"

"No! And I'm horrified to hear it. But you know as well as I do that my wife's diary can be evidence only against herself. Not against me."

"True," Maenmore smiled without amusement. "I have no evidence at all, Mr. Esdale, that you murdered your wife—if that was in your mind."

The Inspector shifted in his chair. Brocker emitted a gasping sigh. Miss Humby gaped at George Esdale for enlightenment, but received none.

"Your somewhat odd behavior with the matches, the document, and the soup could have guilty significance only if it were certain that the poison was placed in the glass *before* the glasses were filled by Mrs. Esdale. That was our first assumption—and a very extravagant assumption too! Suicide or murder, there could have been no certainty that the poison would be taken by the person for whom it was intended." He allowed time for his words to sink in before adding:

"Surely it is more reasonable to assume that the poison was added *after* Mrs. Esdale had distributed the glasses!"

"But who could have added it?" said Miss Humby excitedly. "With the three others looking on?"

"The poison was about half a teaspoonful distilled from a large quantity of Kilfly," said Maenmore. "It was carried in this phial." He held it up for inspection. "We found the phial in the shrubbery of the *front* garden. Which of you three could have thrown it there unobserved?"

"I *could* have," volunteered Brocker. "I opened the french windows and a minute later I went through them, for Dr. Blagrove. But I didn't."

Maenmore glanced at Esdale, who shook his head.

"I'm out of it. I did go to the windows, to shut them and open the panel. My wife asked me to—while she was mixing the drinks at the sideboard. That would have been too early to throw away the phial. After she turned up with the tray, I didn't go near the windows at the front end of the room."

"Miss Humby," said the Chief Constable. "After Mr. Brocker had run for the doctor, you were alone with deceased for a short time, were you not?"

"Yes, but I didn't go near the windows—I was beside her until George came in."

It was an unsupported statement. Maenmore opened a folder containing prints of the photographs taken four hours previously, from which he selected one.

"This photograph shows the settee—empty—and the radio with the cocktail glass on it. Will you look at that, Miss Humby?"

Miss Humby took the photograph, breathing heavily over it.

"After the deceased had placed her own glass on the radio, Miss Humby, she crossed the floor to the bookcase and put down the tray with one glass on it for her husband. Where were you in the room when she was at the bookcase?"

"*Me!*" gasped Miss Humby.

"Gladys," cried George Esdale, "I advise you not to answer that question."

"But, George—"

"Shut up! I'm risking suspension by giving you unsolicited legal advice. Take it. Don't answer any more questions."

"I shall not press Miss Humby for an answer," said the Chief Constable. "Mr. Brocker, where was Miss Humby?"

"Oh, damn! Sorry, Gladys, but there's no escape. Miss Humby went to the radio and removed a book which I had put there when I came in, and she handed the book to me."

"So that Miss Humby—*alone*—had an opportunity to add the poison after the glasses had been distributed. I am not asserting that she did so." He looked at Esdale. "But I am asserting that here is a *prima facie* case. And it is my distasteful duty to take appropriate action."

The Chief Constable stood up. The Inspector followed suit.

"I need not detain you gentlemen any longer. Thank you for the help you have given us."

"George, don't leave me!" Miss Humby clutched at Esdale with both hands. "I don't understand. Does the Colonel think I killed poor Joan? Defend me, George—it's what she would have wished."

"All right, I will defend you." Esdale glanced a question at the Chief Constable, who nodded back. "The Colonel was only stating a case. I can easily smash it. But I shall have to say things you won't like to hear, so you'd better sit in the waiting-room until we're finished." He gripped her by the elbows and marched her to the door. "Gladys, why couldn't you have left that book on the radio? Because you're the most fidgety, interfering little ass in the world! Remember all your life that I have hated you quite a lot. Now get out."

He shut the door behind her and faced the others.

"You guessed what was in that note, Colonel?"

"I didn't *guess*," said Maenmore indignantly. "When I knew you had been in a desperate hurry to burn a document which you yourself had placed on your wife's dressing-table only twenty minutes before, I knew that document was something the police must not be allowed to see. Which meant that you knew the police would come, very soon—*knew it before there was any sign that anything unusual was about to happen!*" He paused. "That document stated that you had committed suicide and that no one must be blamed, and so on."

"Yes, yes!" Esdale's voice was highpitched and excited. "And *that* told you the truth about my gulping that drink?"

"When you gulped that drink you knew that there was one chance in three that it would kill you. That is, the odds were two to one against your being poisoned. You preferred that risk"—he tapped the Report on Scotland Yard—"to odds of nine to one against your escaping conviction."

"All the risk was taken *before* the murder was committed!" cried Esdale. "If the bet came off, I emerged with an absolutely perfect defense. No jury would have believed, after hearing that I gulped down my drink, that I knew there was poison in one of those three glasses before they were handed round."

"If you had been a scoundrel instead of a nervous wreck, Esdale, you'd have got away with it," said Maenmore reflectively. "You wrote that note beforehand because you couldn't stomach the possibility of an innocent person being accused, if it should happen that you received the poison. When you realized that you had not got the glass with the poison, you had to destroy the note before we came. So I knew I had only to produce genuine evidence imperiling one of the innocent persons in order to make you talk."

"Half a minute," said Inspector Rouse. "How could you know it wouldn't kill Mr. Brocker?"

Maenmore answered the question. "He didn't care. The diary shows that those three had got into a tailspin. Esdale was willing to commit the murder of one—*any one*—to prevent the degeneration of the other two—even if it were himself."

"I had the same idea," said Lyle Brocker. "But I dithered."

"*Cor!*" Twenty years of discipline slipped from Inspector Rouse. "She knew one of you two had killed her. But she blamed herself for the set-up and wanted to save the killer!"

"She couldn't save either of us—and she hasn't!" Lyle Brocker said. "George, your odds-on calculation covered only the police risk. You won—but you threw your winnings away, because you wouldn't allow Gladys to be blamed. I get off scot-free—free to walk past your house and listen for your voice. And listen for her voice—year after year!"

*The Case of Poor Gertrude*

# Chapter One

Little more than a century ago we used to pelt hunchbacks with oranges at the circus. As recently as the Edwardian era we were immensely amused by the tragedy of the ageing woman robbed by circumstance of her physiological right to a husband. The havoc wrought in her nervous system, often resulting in a deterioration of manners and a loss of personal dignity, were part of the raw materiel of our music-halls and comic papers. The "old maid" joke got across because everybody knew somebody like that.

One, at least, of these victims of mass-cruelty—the notorious Gertrude Ball—hit back, and with the pitiable device of murder. She made an extraordinarily good job of it, too. The gently nurtured daughter of a rural dean, who had not even read the Sherlock Holmes stories, she danced away from Scotland Yard—baited the police as a matador baits a bull—without the least suspicion that she was being devilishly clever. She had luck—but so, eventually, had the Department of Dead Ends.

In 1908 Gertrude Ball was thirty-five. She lived on the outskirts of the ancient borough of Engeldean in Sussex, with her aunt, Miss Edith Westhorpe. In a small way she was an heiress, for her father had left her over six hundred a year in Consols. Moreover, at twenty she had been reckoned the prettiest girl of her social class in that part of the country. Her photographs show a face that would hold its own today but for the ladylike expression that make so many Edwardian beauties look stupid.

In the earlier twenties she had had one definite engagement and two romantic attachments. None of these, however, had eventuated in marriage. There seemed, in fact, to have been a tendency for her admirers to vanish after the first kiss—though, of course, everything was done in a perfectly nice way.

At thirty she was known as "poor Gertrude," and at thirty-five the more charitable dowagers were protesting that there was still hope, on the ground that miracles had been known to happen. To you this sounds exaggerated, for the truth is that nowadays conventions of dress, hygiene and one thing and another permit a woman to look the age that best suits her temperament. But at that time, if a gentlewoman was thirty-five and unmarried, she took to some genteel hobby that kept her at home.

And then, in the summer of 1908, the dowagers' miracle happened in the person of Wilfred Ankervel—a man in the latter forties, with roots in Engeldean, who had been in Canada for over twenty years, where he had piled up a few thousands as an auctioneer and estate-agent. He was the son of a judge, and had himself been called to the Bar, though he had never tried to practise.

On his return to his native town one can only say that he was seized with love for Gertrude. Suddenly—before they had exchanged a dozen words. But it was not so strange as it now seems, because Gertrude, by blind chance, happened to bear a remarkable physical resemblance to Ankervel's dead wife, whom he had loved exceedingly. The ghost of her gestures, the echo of her voice stampeded him.

Ankervel arrived in the middle of August. In September, in the presence of her aunt, he proposed. Gertrude accepted with calm dignity and even made a stipulation—that whenever he was not actually engaged in his calling he should describe himself as a barrister-at-law. This, she felt, they both owed to the late rural dean.

It will be difficult for you to realize the enormous difference made in the life of such a woman by the right to wear a half-hoop of diamonds on the third finger of her left hand. From a person to whom one was over-civil for fear of hurting her susceptibilities, whom one rarely met outside the social functions of the church, she became the inspiration of a round of picnics, dinner-parties, garden-at-homes, and the like.

Ankervel treated her with a reverence that was very nearly

ridiculous. But everyone assumed that it was a Canadian custom and thought it rather charming.

Ankervel had come straight back to the house of his late father, and had installed an elderly housekeeper in charge of two youngish servants. Convention permitted Gertrude to take tea with him as often as he liked. It must have been on one of these occasions that she became aware that he kept a loaded revolver in a little wall safe, together with his mother's jewelry, which would be Gertrude's on their wedding-day.

At his house—in October—she consented to name the day, November 27th following. He was, we may assume, so entranced with her compliance that he laid aside some of the reverence and for the first time kissed her, as a man kisses the woman he wants to marry.

The kiss, she records in her diary, took place as the clock was striking five on a sunny afternoon. ("*We did not speak after this as I think our hearts were too full. I went out into the garden and in a minute Wilfred was by my side. He was so silent that I was afraid I had lowered myself in his eyes. On the way home through the woods, as we were passing the old quarry, he touched my arm. I am sure it was by intention. I shall always love the old quarry and shall not allow him to have it cleared. Aunt E. is going to post the invitations at once. I do hope people won't send expensive presents. I am so happy.*")

That little rhapsody was entered in her diary on 3rd October, 1908. Strangely—or not—it echoes an entry in her diary of 1902—the year of the second of the 'romantic attachments.' She records the kiss, followed by the slightly puzzling silence of the man, which she interprets: '*His heart was too full to put into words the pledge which his act had already given.*' Meaning that, having kissed her he would inevitably propose marriage. As we know, he did not. In effect, he never spoke to her again.

Nothing much seems to have happened in the week following Ankervel's kiss except that the invitations to the wedding were sent. The lovers met, but only for short intervals and, as it happened, in the presence of Miss Westhorpe. This might be accounted for by the fact that Ankervel had decided to buy a partnership in Harshalt's, an old-established local firm of auctioneers and estate-agents. She did not see him at all on Sunday, for he had to spend a duty weekend with some relatives at Cheltenham.

On Monday, October 9th, there occurred the incident of the dream, which subsequently gave the case much of its notoriety. At about four in the morning Annie, the house-parlormaid, heard screams coming from Miss Ball's room. She rushed in, getting there a few seconds before Miss Westhorpe, to find Miss Ball in tears.

"Oh, Annie, I've had such an awful nightmare!" she exclaimed. "I dreamt that I had killed Mr. Ankervel and buried him in the old quarry."

So that was all! Miss Westhorpe gave the necessary soothing replies.

On Tuesday morning there were no screams. But when her aunt taxed her at breakfast with her tired appearance, Gertrude admitted that she had had the dream a second time. Her aunt dutifully laughed it away, though this time she felt a little creepy. A modern aunt would probably have been more alarmed. For an aunt nowadays knows the elements of psychology and might have inferred that in her subconsciousness Gertrude already knew how it was between her and her lover and had determined upon her remedy.

That night Ankervel, having returned from Cheltenham, dined with them, and they told him the story of the dream. He smiled with male superiority, made a joke or two, and forgot it. He left early, excusing himself on the ground that his cousins had kept him up until the small hours every night. He did not see Gertrude alone, but asked her to come to tea at his house the following afternoon.

It was then that he told her, as gently as he could, that he had made a tragic mistake, which must necessarily blight the lives of both of them.

"Of the two abominable courses open to me, I feel that the less cruel, the less dishonorable, is to tell you. . . . A week ago I could have doubted there was a sun in the sky as easily as I could have doubted that I love you. Now—God forgive me, Gertrude!—I esteem you above all women, but I have to ask you to release me from our engagement."

No reason given! And poor Gertrude—as the dowagers would again be calling her—asked for none.

"Of course, Wilfred!" Twenty years of the discipline of the drawing-room held her steady. "I shall always respect and admire you for speaking to me frankly and giving me the chance to be worthy of your friendship."

Ornate, you will say, and artificial! And, if you like, horribly insincere! But there is a sort of sincerity in good manners, which the Edwardians understood. He was immensely grateful to her for running true to form. Not, of course, that he had really expected her to brawl or sue him for breach of promise. But there it was.

"Please leave all arrangements to me," she asked. "Aunt Edith will cancel the invitations."

We imagine that he groaned heavily.

"Not the least of the suffering I have brought upon you will be the tittle-tattle of those infernal old women!"

Oh, no, not the least by a long way! And not only the old women, but the young women. And the men. The very errand-boys would know about it and snigger. The marriage was suitable in every material and social sense. But the man had escaped while he could.

"Gertrude, you must, of course, allow me to announce that you have broken our engagement on account of an incident in my past life, which need need not be specified."

As if anyone would believe that!

"No—no! I will not have you vilify yourself, Wilfred. Our—our friendship has meant too much to me," she said, and possibly believed it. And then: "If you are anxious to spare me I ask you, if you will, to say and do nothing for a few days. Just give me a little time in which to adjust myself. And, if you have no objection, let us behave—in public—as if nothing had happened."

Anything she liked, of course! It was a faintly eccentric request, but it was not for him to cavil, after the way he had been unfortunately compelled to treat her. And after she had been so perfectly ripping about it.

"Just as you like! I will do nothing whatever. I intend to go back to Canada, of course. I shall sell this place and back out of the Harshalt deal, But I will do nothing whatever until you announce that our engagement is at an end. May I see you home, Gertrude?"

When she got home Gertrude said she had a bad headache, and went to bed. There, we may assume, she had a good look at her future. She would again be helping with the Church decorations at Christmas. "Poor Gertrude" once more, she would have to endure the dreadful patronage of the dowagers, less friendly now, because they would feel they had been fooled. Next winter she would again be a wallflower at the Hunt Ball—would know again the subtle agony of having no partner for the supper dance. ("*Poor Gertrude! she had four chances altogether, but each time the man backed out for some reason or other. I rather fancy there must be something about her....*")

No. Those three earlier affairs were nothing. The fourth man was madly in love with her. The wedding-day was fixed and then—

She would have to give him back his ring. She removed it and put it in its little padded jeweler's case. "The London and Montreal Jewelry Co., Ltd." She had never heard of them. No doubt the name had attracted a man fresh from Canada. Dear Wilfred was not very original-minded. The ring itself was a perfectly conventional half-hoop of very fine diamonds.

But it was her ring. It had been her apotheosis and she loved it for itself. She could not bear to part with it. But her own code demanded that she give it back.

With no other thought than that she must have the outward and visible sign of it to console her in secret in the blank years to come she went alone the next morning to town—to the London and Montreal Jewelry Co. Here she enquired about a half-hoop in imitation stones. "My fiancé quite agrees that my engagement ring is too valuable for daily wear." The assistant produced an illustrated price-list and recommended design 62 in "good paste." Price sixteen pounds. Indistinguishable from the real thing save by an expert.

Assured of her unassailable position, she tendered a cheque which was accepted after they had verified her name and address.

On the afternoon of the next day she again went to Wilfred's house.

"I have had time to adjust my thoughts, Wilfred," she told him after tea. "Tonight I will ask Aunt Edith to put an announcement in *The Times* and we shall both write to a few friends ... Your ring."

Looking just a little like Ellen Terry in *Cormorant*, she drew it from her finger. He received it with becoming gravity and placed it on the mantelpiece—which, somehow, was too much for her.

"No—no! Lock it away, Wilfred, so that no one can see it," she begged. Now we are entitled to believe that this was the spontaneous expression of her tortured nerves—that there was no dreadful thought behind it. For we know that she had put on her gloves in readiness to go. It is at least certain that she had not at that moment decided how she would murder him—if indeed her full consciousness had decided to murder him at all. We may believe that she was enticed by circumstance.

He opened the wall-safe and put the ring with the other jewelry, and before he shut the safe he blushed and apologized.

"Forgive me. I am very remiss." He pulled from his waistcoat pocket a gold sovereign purse—a common little device that presented each gold coin separately by means of a spring. It had been her engagement present to him and, of course, he wore it on his watch-chain. Three clicks—as he removed three sovereigns from the case and put them in his pocket.

With his fingers he could not prize open the link attaching the sovereign purse to his watchchain. So he went into the hall for a pair of pliers.

While he was away she took his revolver from the safe and hid it in her muff.

"Perhaps—er—I had better send this by post?"

"There is no need for you to do that," she answered him. She took the sovereign purse in her left hand, in which she was already holding her handkerchief.

"Will you see me home, Wilfred—for the last time? Let's take the upper path through the woods."

The upper path runs over the crest of the hill and passes near the old quarry. She took him to the verge of the thirty-foot precipice from which there *is* a view of Engeldean nestling in the valley—a fact which, in the circumstances, lent itself to a little melancholy sentimentalizing.

But it was a chilly evening and she sneezed. As she was about to apply her handkerchief, the gold sovereign purse fell at her feet. There was a moment of mutual confusion in which her foot tipped the sovereign purse so that it rolled over the edge of the little cliff.

"How stupid of me! Don't let us bother about it," she entreated. In a sense, she really was entreating him to save her against herself. But it was of no use.

"We can be down there in five minutes," he protested. "There's plenty of light and I have marked the spot."

The precipitous face of the stone, a semicircle cut from the side of the hill, was about a hundred yards from the lower path. In the foreground were boulders, loose stones and nettles and a great deal of rubbish. Over this they clambered together.

In a rough trench beneath the cliff-face Ankervel caught the gleam of the sovereign purse and stooped to pick it up.

As he was rising Gertrude shot him through the back of the head, and flung the revolver into a cavity in the cliff face.

At about a quarter to six—it was now October the 13th, 1908—Miss Westhorpe was in the hall, when her niece returned.

"Oh, there you are, dear? It's early for a muff, isn't it, though I see Lady Maynton has started hers. Isn't Wilfred coming in for a few minutes?"

"I'm so afraid of getting my chilblains again—it isn't fair to Wilfred to take such a risk. No. He left me at the edge of the woods. He has to write a couple of business letters and then he's coming to dinner. I told him we shouldn't dress tonight—just a cosy little evening, Aunt Edith."

Miss Westhorpe remembered every detail of this conversation, though at the time it made no impression, except that she gave the necessary orders in the kitchen.

They waited dinner half an hour for Wilfred Ankervel, then sat down without him.

(*"My niece was a little hurt at first, which I thought only natural in the circumstances," testified Miss Westhorpe on a later occasion. "After dinner she suddenly remembered her dream and wanted to send a maid with a note to inquire whether anything had happened to him. I am afraid I was responsible for persuading her that her fears must be groundless."*)

On the following morning there was neither explanation nor apology from Wilfred Ankervel, so Miss Westhorpe herself ordered the pony-trap and drove to Ankervel's house to make inquiries.

"No, Miss Westhorpe, he didn't come home after he left the house with Miss Ball. But he'd said he might have to go up to London suddenly—and he had some luggage sent down to the station in the morning, so I didn't worry."

The information, in the light of the other three gentlemen who loved and rode away, made Miss Westhorpe uneasy, and she was not sensibly relieved by the way her niece took the news.

"Something has happened to him!" she cried, climbing into the pony-trap. "I'm going for help—I'm going to the police. I tell you, Aunt Edith, I *feel* something has happened."

Her aunt saw that a great deal of talk, at any rate, was going to happen. She could do nothing to restrain her niece, who took the reins and whipped up the pony. In the town they met more than one of their acquaintances to whom Gertrude, with an abandon rare in those days, shouted: "Something has happened to Wilfred—I'm going to the police." Lady Maynton, who was a liberal subscriber to police charities, actually followed them into the police station.

Superintendent Lordways listened politely and then, being an efficient officer, sent a man to the nearby railway station to inquire about the luggage. Presently they learnt that two cabin trunks had been sent, luggage in advance, to the Overseas Club in London. They were unable to say for certain whether Mr. Ankervel had gone up on the evening train, as his ticket had been taken that morning.

"Until we know Mr. Ankervel's movements in London," said the Superintendent, "we've no reason to fear that anything out of the ordinary must have happened."

"Quite so, Mr. Lordways!—that is exactly what I would have said myself," remarked Lady Maynton. And she smiled. And Gertrude saw her smile.

When they had gone Superintendent Lordways stepped across to Mr. Harshalt's offices and asked him whether he could give any information about the man who was believed to be already his partner. Harshalt wanted to know full details and as he heard them he pricked up his ears.

"That's a very funny thing, Lordways," he remarked. "Between you and me, Lordways, Mr. Ankervel has been very queer the last few days. A week ago he was hurrying up the solicitors to produce the draft of our agreement. But when the agreement arrived on Monday, he steadily made excuses for not signing it. There's been no hitch on the business side of it. I couldn't understand it. I wondered whether—very strictly between you and me, Lordways—I wondered whether he contemplated making some change in—er—his personal plans."

Lordways thanked him and departed and scrupulously avoided talking about it to anybody. But Harshalt talked quite a lot about it, repeated all Lordways had said and all that he had said, with the obvious embellishments.

That afternoon Miss Westhorpe went alone to Mrs. Graigie's at-home. When she got back Gertrude had gone to bed with another headache. At breakfast next morning Gertrude asked:

"What were the people saying at Mrs. Graigie's?"

"I can't possibly tell you," said her aunt—but of course she could, when she was properly pressed to do so. "They're saying he has run away from you," she sobbed.

"Then mark my words. Aunt Edith, they shall apologize to me—for the rest of their lives." Gertrude was fierce—and dreadfully impatient to make them apologize. Her impatience drove her to put her head into the lion's mouth. That afternoon—at the police station.

To Gertrude the police were nice, respectful men like good servants, and the Superintendent was a sort of butler to whom one could unbend without loss of dignity.

"I tell you Mr. Ankervel is dead," she asserted. "I'm as sure of it as if I could see him lying at my feet in this room. I dreamt of it last night. Twice before I have had a similar dream—only before I dreamt that I killed him myself and buried him." And as the Superintendent blinked: "That means, of course, that there was a danger coming to him from which I ought to have protected him."

Now the Superintendent had picked up Mr. Harshalt's hint and in his heart he did not take any serious notice of her. In the end she virtually ordered him to search Mr. Ankervel's woods and out of respect for her late father he gallantly consented to take a couple of men and look round.

In the woods they spent a couple of hours beating the undergrowth on either side of the path without result. It was a messy business, for a fortnight's drought had been broken by heavy rain during the night.

"I don't think we shall find anything here," said Gertrude. "In two of my dreams the body was in the old quarry."

The police were tired and wholly incredulous. But this implacable little old maid with nerves of steel made them beat amongst the boulders and nettles of the old quarry while she hovered on the pathway.

"Nothing here, miss."

"You haven't looked at the back. Oh, please do look properly! I'm sure I'm right!" she shrilled.

There in the rough trench they found the body of Wilfred Ankervel—found, too, the revolver, which they promptly wrapped in a silk handkerchief.

They let Gertrude know they had found him and that he was dead.

"I knew, I knew!" she said and cried a little. While the

Superintendent was trying to comfort her, one of the men called out:

"There's something in his hand, sir, and I can't open the fingers."

"Use the flat of your jack-knife as a lever. I'm coming."

They levered open the dead fingers and found the gold sovereign purse, empty, slightly dented.

When they reported the find to Gertrude, her strength gave out and she fainted—which the police thought very womanly and appropriate.

That night the Chief Constable called in Scotland Yard, and Detective Inspector Drayling came down.

"You took it that he had gone up to Town to run away from this girl? And you did nothing about it. The next thing is, the girl takes you by the scruff of the neck and rubs your nose in the murder. And she tells you she dreamt it all. Unluckily for me, my Chief never listens when I tell him about people's dreams. Where does Miss Ball live?"

Drayling was with her for a couple of hours and there can be little doubt that she derived a perverted pleasure from the interview. She had started to come home, she said, with Mr. Ankervel at about five. He had left her at the edge of the wood, she said, in order to go back and write a couple of business letters, after which he was to come to her house for dinner. He cross-examined her and gained nothing, but her approval of his thoroughness. She was positively eager to give him her fingerprints.

"Whatever you say, Inspector," she warned him, "I shall always blame myself. I ought to have made him understand his danger. I must tell you that I had a dream—"

Drayling had to listen to the dream. She called in Miss Westhorpe to give her version of the dream and then Annie, the house-parlourmaid.

That night, in spite of his boast, Drayling was compelled to feature the dream in his report to his superiors.

Before he wrote the report he went to Ankervel's house, where he learnt that the deceased had kept a revolver in the wall-safe, so it might be tentatively assumed that he had been shot with his own weapon. It was just possible, he found out, for Miss Ball to have got at that weapon. So, for that matter, could the housekeeper. So, assuming a little simple trickery, could almost anyone. Nothing there.

He rang up Ankervel's solicitor, learnt that a will was being drafted, to be signed by Ankervel after marriage, leaving everything to his intended wife. Ankervel had therefore died intestate. Nothing there. The next day he went back to the old quarry.

Where had Ankervel been shot? On the path? Impossible to say, for the rain had washed away all traces.

Had he been shot in the trench? At the foot of the precipice where the body was found? If so, how had he happened to be there at the time of the shooting? Some hundred yards from the path. A most unnatural place for a man to loiter in at about six on an autumn evening. He had not been shot above the precipice and dropped over—the doctor had been firm about that.

Well, then, he must have been carried dead to that trench, or enticed there alive. But not by his girl—it was a dirty and uncomfortable spot. And besides, they were not that class.

Miss Ball, he reluctantly decided, must be ruled out of it. A decision which was strengthened by the information that the fingerprints on the revolver were not those of Miss Ball—that they were, in fact, the fingerprints of one George Byker, a petty sneak-thief who had served several short terms of imprisonment.

At the inquest Gertrude told her tale, simple and unshakable—not that anyone tried to shake it. The sovereign purse, slightly dented, was among the exhibits. She identified it as a present given by herself to the deceased. The local jeweler from whom she had bought it confirmed this statement. There was the romantic suggestion that Ankervel had died defending his fiancée's gift, which was quite enough for the jury to return a verdict of "willful murder against a person unknown."

Gertrude gave her evidence well and everyone in Court felt keen sympathy for the tragic little woman who seemed to face her bereavement with an almost fierce resignation. It occurred to no one that the same tragic little figure might be burning with hatred, against those whose mockery had driven her to the immolation of her conscience. She left the Court on the arm of her aunt, and for several days kept to her bed.

On the day after the inquest the dragnet brought in George Byker.

He was a semi-defective tramp whose original home was in Lewes. His movements were traced to the vicinity of Engeldean at an essential time. From Engeldean he took the train to London on the day following the murder and paid his fare with a gold sovereign. He bought clothes and boots at a second-hand store in Praed Street, also tendering a sovereign. That night he was run in for being drunk and disorderly, and the following morning was fined ten shillings, which again he paid in gold.

He was charged with the murder of Wilfred Ankervel and in due course was committed for trial.

For the defense it was stated that he had spent the night in the quarry, which he knew of old, arriving there at about ten at night. In the morning he was startled to see a corpse lying in the trench and a revolver in a cavity close by. He had picked up the revolver, had handled it a little before putting it back where he had found it. He was afraid to tell the police of his discovery, in view of his record, and he admitted that he had gone through the pockets of the corpse and taken out three pounds in gold and two shillings in silver.

The prosecution suggested that Byker had accosted Ankervel and attempted to grab his watch, possessing himself of the sovereign purse. There was a scuffle in which the sovereign purse rolled to the ground and was trodden on, being crushed against a stone, Ankervel then drew his revolver, threatening the prisoner with it, until he was able to pick up the sovereign purse. Taking Ankervel unawares, the prisoner succeeded in snatching the revolver, whereupon Ankervel ran and hid in the trench, where the prisoner found and shot him. Alternatively, the prisoner might have shot the deceased on the path and carried the body to the trench.

The jury did not bother about such subtleties. A man who would admittedly rob a dead man's body would be capable of anything.

After a short retirement they found the prisoner guilty of murder and, possibly because they had been a little hasty, added a recommendation to mercy on account of his feeble intelligence. The judge sentenced him to death and forwarded the recommendation, which was accepted by the Home Secretary, with the result that George Byker went to penal servitude for life.

Gertrude Ball, the gently nurtured daughter of a rural dean, again identified the sovereign purse and again told the simple, unshakable little lie about her own and Ankervel's movements. Counsel for the Prosecution, in thanking her, expressed sympathy on account of her bereavement; the Court associated itself. Gertrude, in short, emerged a popular heroine.

She did not attend the Hunt Ball. But in the spring she went into half-mourning and was occasionally seen at the more important at-homes. She was still "poor Gertrude," but the phrase now had a totally different ring. The dowagers were friendly and confidential, conferring a kind of honorary wifehood upon her. It was considered very appropriate and even rather beautiful that she continued to wear her engagement ring, over a mourning ring.

Altogether she had become a very interesting figure. In the summer she was occasionally seen at tennis parties, though she never played. "Such a sad, beautiful face," someone had said, so she never smiled, except sadly. The girls asked her advice as an honorary dowager. Gertrude had found her niche and was happy—while George Byker settled down more or less comfortably at Dartmoor.

The London and Montreal Jewelry Co., Ltd., had passed from an old-fashioned father to an ultra-modern son, who tied himself up rather tightly with a Gaiety girl of the wrong sort.

She had soon absorbed all the legitimate profits of the business, with the indirect result that the accounts and records of the firm were taken charge of by the Public Prosecutor.

Rason, of the Department of Dead Ends, was looking through their Special List (in the hope of finding something about the Lowestoft polygamist) when his eye was caught by the entry:

*Ball, Gertrude, Miss, The Lindens, Mr. Engeldean, Ring (62), £16, cheque, Oct. 12th, 1908.*

He looked up Ring 62 in their price list: 'Paste half-hoop. Ideal and original engagement ring.'

One of these had been bought by Gertrude Ball on—yes—*on the day before the murder of her fiancé!* On the face of it there was no connection between the two facts. Rason set about the job of making one.

"Never mind about the murder for a moment. Why does an engaged woman buy herself an engagement ring? Because the man is too hard up to buy it for her? But this man was not hard up for sixteen pounds. Then why?"

Presently Rason turned up the report of the trial, found among other things that she had given him a gold sovereign purse. But surely she hadn't also given him a paste ring? One never knows. Better make sure.

Ankervel having died intestate, Rason obtained leave from the proper official in Chancery to inspect the jewelry, most of which had originally been the property of Ankervel's mother. Here he saw the sovereign purse, with a dent in it. Then a diamond half-hoop. Comparing it with the illustrated price-list, he was astonished to find what was apparently the very same 'ideal and original engagement ring.'

Rason took it slowly. Of course, the ring might have belonged to Ankervel's mother. He glanced again at the price list. No—that was not the sort of jewelry that stayed in a family—it was admittedly paste.

Very well, then! A young lady gives her fiancé, of all things under the sun, a gemmed engagement ring! Buys it the day before her fiancé is murdered. No link-up. Unless—

On the way down to Engeldean, the price list in one pocket, the sovereign purse in another, he thought up a good excuse for troubling Miss Ball, but in the event he did not use it. He was too electrified to see on that lady's hand, above a mourning ring, another exact replica of Engagement Ring No. 62.

He talked some gibberish about the London and Montreal Co. while he felt his way. They were alone together in the morning-room.

Rason decided to take a risk. He looked fixedly at the ring until she winced and then:

"Before I go any further, Miss Ball, I think it only fair to tell you that we know you bought that ring yourself. You paid for it with a cheque for sixteen pounds on October the 12th."

"*Oh!*" The fierce little spinster who had twice committed perjury without a tremor collapsed in tears. "Oh—the humiliation!" she sobbed. "It's true—I admit it! But it's not a crime, Mr. Rason—need you tell anyone? You will make me the laughing-stock of the county. I could never hold up my head again. You will ruin my whole life."

Rason thought of the luckless tramp in Dartmoor and went hard as flint.

"You bought the ring for yourself—a duplicate of the one Mr. Ankervel gave you—because you had to give him back the original one? *Because he had ended your engagement?*"

"Yes." In a broken whisper Gertrude admitted the shameful, unforgivable truth that a man had rejected her love. "I was a coward. I couldn't bear people to know that he had—had jilted me as if I had been a servant-girl."

Rason saw where he was now and the rest was easy.

"You paid sixteen pounds for that ring. . . . What use would the ring have been to you—*if Wilfred Ankervel had lived?*"

It was a simple question, but it was wholly unanswerable. Rason repeated it and while he was waiting for the answer that never came, he realized that George Byker had told the truth at his trial. And he remembered that dent in the sovereign purse.

"That ring would have been no use at all if Ankervel had lived. So you shot him yourself. You lured him to that spot by dropping the sovereign purse over the cliff—"

But Miss Ball had positively stamped her foot.

"Mr. Rason, will you have the goodness to stop! I do not care to have such things discussed—still less will I allow them to be published." To Rason it looked very like hysteria, but it was nothing of the kind. "I plead guilty to murdering Mr. Ankervel. And I would be obliged if you would say nothing whatever about the circumstances. I shall not mention them myself. And there will, of course, be no trial."

A fragment of legal knowledge which, we may assume, she acquired from the one-time barrister-at-law. She signed a three-line confession, repeated it to the judge and in four minutes was sentenced to death—leaving half her property to her aunt and the other half to George Byker. Engeldean made a totally erroneous guess at the nature of the "felonious malice aforethought."

*No Women Asked*

# Chapter One

From the official point of view, the murder in the *Astarte* was one of those delightful things that simply can't happen twice. There was no running about: not a single motor car was employed on either side: there were no telephone calls. The corpse was delivered at the doors of Scotland Yard and—in the same parcel, as it were—all the witnesses and the very 'scene of the crime' itself, complete with fingerprints, footprints and four red-hot suspects.

This somewhat unusual effect was contrived by no one. It came about as the result of intelligent, law-abiding persons behaving as sensibly as they could in the circumstances of the murder, in itself an unsophisticated affair, accomplished with a carving knife. The oddity—even if it is an oddity of outline only—was due to the unbalancing personality of Mabel Rouse.

There have always been women like Mabel, often cropping up in other people's Memoirs. They are those kind-hearted, unreliable women of no importance—not clever and not as physically gorgeous as they make you think they are—who distort the perspective of able men, including policemen. Detective Inspector Kyle, though himself undisturbed by her physical presence, was aware of her pervasive genius impeding his investigation and throwing the normal procedure out of gear.

The crime thrust itself upon the police on a very hot afternoon in a very hot summer. On Waterloo Bridge many pedestrians stopped to admire the motor boat, *Astarte*, as it passed under the bridge on its way up-stream. When the boat was within hailing distance of Westminster Pier, its horn sounded. A waterman came out of the shed which was the public waiting room and observed the boat, admiring its general air of expensiveness—he was almost ready to call it a yacht. Upwards of fifty feet on the water-line, he guessed. Built for river and coastal cruising—to the owner's design, by the look of it—with more beam than you'd expect, and a railed deck on the roof. One man control, too! Money!

The launch approached to within six feet of the pier, then held itself against the current. The skipper and owner was a man in the early thirties. He was clad in a pull-over, an open shirt and flannels; his hair was rumpled, and his lean face was moist, but a certain elegance persisted. He bent over the steering and spoke to the pier hand.

"I want you to run across the road to Scotland Yard." He was not shouting: his voice had the pitch and clarity of the trained speaker. He lobbed a cigar box, which the other caught. "Give them the envelope in that box. The ten bob wrapped round the envelope is yours. Please be as quick as you can."

With a glance at the door of the saloon, which was shut, the skipper moved from the pier, crossed the river and began to potter about, to kill time. It would take the waterman, say, a minute to work his way across the road. At the Yard, a few minutes might be lost before the note was read by an official with authority to act. Another three or four minutes for the machinery to start. Call it ten minutes, all told.

The envelope, marked 'very urgent', was addressed to the 'Chief Inspector or Deputy.' Within two minutes it was opened by Detective Inspector Kyle.

The note paper was embossed '*Astarte.*'

> *A murder has been committed on this launch. I am off Westminster Pier and will put in on signal from you with white handkerchief waved at shoulder level. George Broughby (owner).*

Kyle, an ascetic bachelor, had the appearance of a prosperous business man with a large family of daughters. He never rushed anything. He blinked at the note, then swivelled in his chair and reached for Lloyd's register. '*Astarte:* owner, George Broughby.' Good! Ninety seconds later he had learnt that George Broughby was thirty-five, unmarried, chairman of Broughby Tyres Ltd., founded by his father, and that he owned a racing stable. He rang for Sergeant Dobson and gave instructions, with special reference to heading off sightseers.

Within eleven minutes of reading Broughby's note, Kyle was on the pier. Beside him stood Sergeant Dobson, two plain clothes men in the rear. There were two uniformed constables on the Embankment and a dozen standing by at the Yard. The team of technical men was due to report on the pier in ten minutes.

The *Astarte* was idling on the Surrey side. Kyle waved a white handkerchief at shoulder level. The launch crossed the river at half speed. At a nod from Broughby the waterman made fast.

"I am Detective Inspector Kyle."

"My name is Broughby. Come aboard, please."

# Chapter Two

The *Astarte* had sailed from Chiswick that morning, the intention being to run down the river to the Southend regatta. George Broughby was giving a small birthday party. Mabel's birthday, of course. Her twenty-eighth, she said, and like most of her positive statements this was very nearly true.

Mabel was 'resting.' In this phase of her life she was, in a sense, an actress—though perhaps 'artiste' is a safer word. As 'Cherry Dane' she sometimes played very small parts on the stage and bit parts in films, but most of her engagements were in cabaret. That she could do an acceptable floor show turn, however witless, was due to an infectious vitality—an effervescence of contradictory qualities, echoed in her physical appearance.

The lines of her were of near showgirl standard. She had coppery-chestnut hair with bright blue eyes, a slightly tilted nose and a mouth wide enough to awaken surmise. Her natural color clash was carefully developed in her dress. A green jumper fought with a tartan skirt which owed less to Scotland than to Hollywood: her stockings maintained neutrality: her black shoes had green buckles—and she absorbed it all into a vivid unit that was herself. Her voice was a veiled contralto which so often lent her banalities the timbre of an intimate confession.

In her character she was acquisitive without being mercenary. She would never bestow herself for money, though she contrived to love, with some frequency, where money abounded.

She cheated nobody but herself. Her ex-lovers remained her staunch friends, holding her in a kind of family affection. She created her own social atmosphere, which would have been acceptable almost anywhere if she had wished to make it so.

First aboard that morning had been Mabel herself. One boarded the *Astarte* at the wheel-house, which was a little aft: forward was the saloon, with a companionway to the deck, the floor of the deck being the roof of the saloon. She turned aft and opened a door giving on to a corridor.

On her left—she could never think in terms of port and starboard—was the galley, which she called the kitchenette, fitted with a small electric cooker and a large refrigerator, a waste bin and a basket for unwashed crockery and table utensils. On the right of the corridor were two guest cabins, containing bunks—beyond these, a bathroom-toilet, tiled and fitted with a shower bath.

Again on her left, next to the galley, was a single cabin nearly as large as the two guest cabins together: beyond it, opposite the bathroom, were lockers which she called cupboards. From one of the latter she took a full-length overall, a duster and a chamois cloth.

The nearly double-size cabin was Mabel's. She pushed back the sliding door. The cabin made few concessions to maritime prejudice, having the general appearance of a bedroom in the London flat of a fastidious woman. True that the legs of the bed were screwed to the floor, as were those of the dressing table, while the wardrobe, with full-length mirror, was built in.

On the bevel of the mirror she was happy to find a little dust overlooked by the staff that serviced the *Astarte* by contract. It justified the duster, which was less an article of equipment than a symbol of the domesticity for which she honestly believed herself to crave. With any luck she would find a job for the chamois. Presently, she went forward, past the wheelhouse, down the companionway to the saloon.

Here again Mabel's influence was instantly discernible in the unusual liberality of floor space. It was possible to walk about without wriggling or even dodging: the tallest man could stand erect not only under the superstructure that gave a centre light, but everywhere else. There were two divan-settees and two heavy armchairs, besides easy chairs of upholstered wicker. An escritoire was flanked by a television console and a cocktail cabinet. There was no centre table; but one could be conjured up in a few minutes by means of a system of interlocking occasional tables, the legs fitting into sockets in the floor.

Mabel was putting an extra sheen on the cocktail glasses when George Broughby came aboard.

For a dozen years, George Broughby had frustrated matchmaking mothers, without deeply offending one of them. He positively bristled with eligibilities of position and even of person. The inner conflicts of his temperament did not meet the eye. He was too intelligent to interfere with the successful management of Broughby Tyres and it was not easy to find employment for his talents elsewhere. He had grown tired of the toys still provided for a rich man until he had chanced upon Mabel. He had snatched her, to discover, too late, that she was not a toy at all—though she herself believed that she could not be anything else.

He had been hurrying. But when he entered the saloon he stood silent, watching her intently, as if he were trying to reassess her.

"I've nearly finished!" she said without looking up. "George, I heard you talking on the 'phone to Harold Crendon—who is the American he's bringing along?"

"I don't know. Hold everything for a minute and listen. That fellow who came to the flat this morning as you left was the Party agent. They've adopted me as candidate for Charbury. I'm to go down on Tuesday and speak."

"How perfectly splendid, George!" She had turned herself into a shimmering figure of delight. "It's what you wanted more than anything." Therefore, for the moment, it was what she herself wanted more than anything.

"If I get in at the bye-election, it's a beginning, even if it's only the beginning of a flop. But there's a snag. My fault—I was a fool to let 'em have our address. To cut it short, the agent didn't say he knew we were not married, but he made it quite clear that, if I am to represent Charbury in Parliament—"

"I'll have all my things out of that flat by midday tomorrow."

"Don't interrupt so, Mabel! Before I left, I 'phoned the firm's solicitors to get a special license so that we can be married right away."

A small sound escaped from Mabel, which Broughby did not know to be a moan of frustration. Here was the call back to the comfort, security and respectability which she had thrown away six years ago but had now learnt to value. And the call had to come today!

"That is, if you will," added Broughby. "You will marry me, won't you? Of course you will!"

She was not yet sure that it was more than a passing notion of his.

"All my life, George dear, I shall remember with happiness that you asked me. But—"

"'Angel voices off-stage'!" snorted Broughby. "It's a practical proposition."

Still cautious, she began to look at it from his angle. It was part of her genius that she could say to a man the sort of things his mother would have said to him.

"It isn't practical to marry a woman with a past, as my father politely called it."

"But you have been frank—and that takes the sting out of it. You can make a job of a politician's wife, if you put your mind to it. Your stage experience will come in useful. Self-possession. No blushing and stammering in public. Besides, what am I to do when I come home if you aren't there?"

He had worked it all out in a couple of minutes before ringing for the special license. He had faced the drawbacks and made his decision. He had not guessed that she might be the one to hesitate.

"George darling! You're giving a birthday party for me. You have asked men only. Because you don't like the only kind of women you could ask to meet me."

"We could ask any kind of women if we were married." He glanced with distaste at the wedding ring on her finger which he had bought and handed to her in a taxi.

"It would mean such a change for us both," she objected, half-heartedly. "Let's make a tremendous effort to be sensible about each other—and tomorrow we'll say goodbye without regrets on either side."

Regrets? Possibly not. Instead, a gnawing ache in the nervous system—a shabby kind of self-reproach that he had thrown away a bubbling essence of vitality that was beyond good and evil, stupidity and wisdom. Her lovers of the past meant nothing—her imagined lovers of the future were already torturing him with their laughter at the fool who preferred mouthing platitudes from a platform.

"Don't choose for me, Mabel. I know what I'm doing. You're safe with drink. You know when not to make a blue joke. And—if if you want me to say it—I'd miss you like hell!"

Because he had been a hell of a long time finding her. She was an awful little vulgarian, in some ways. But she had given him a kind of friendship which he had glimpsed at Eton, missed at Magdalen and had given up hope of attaining in London. She nourished his self-confidence, leaving him uncomfortably dependent upon her.

"What about it?" he demanded.

Evidently, he had thought out the objections and knew his own mind. She must play for time—only a very little time. Until her suspicions of Crendon's American were settled one way or the other.

"Please! My head is full of the party—six of us, all told, unless you've asked anybody else? Give me till tomorrow morning, George—and let's go on today as if nothing had happened."

"All right! When the license turns up I shall carry you along and if you don't want to go through with it, you can tell 'em when we get there."

George really wanted to marry her. For a moment, that thought filled her universe.

"Will you take some chairs on deck, George? I can manage the drinks."

"I have to see the boathouse manager. The others will be here at any minute. They'll like to be asked to do a job o' work."

She finished the cocktail glasses and checked them. Six—including herself and the unknown American. If he was unknown! She began to arrange flowers in a copper bowl which clashed with her hair. Her hands were trembling, but she steadied when she heard a footstep. Charles Hardelow was the first arrival.

Hardelow was a chartered accountant, a partner in his father's firm at the expensive end of Victoria Street. He was a sleek little man who could not help looking tailored, even when wearing flannels and a blazer. Kindly, generous, easy-going, he had the air of being bullied by his gardener and mothered by his wife. Yet he had dared brilliantly and had won from Mabel an experience on which his imagination would feed for the rest of his life.

"Charlie! How lovely to see you again!" Mabel kissed him on the cheek. "Marriage is good for you, dear—d'you know you've come over all chubby?"

"Can't fight heredity!" Even his voice was the voice of a man who treasures his normality and will eventually be fat. "And you are as much of a sylph as ever."

"How can you tell, through this overall? Charlie, who is the American Harold Crendon is bringing?"

"First I've heard of him. I haven't brought you a birthday present."

"Never mind! If you're hard up, I can do something for you." She might yet fall between two stools and could lose nothing by building up reserves. She hurried on: "I've got hold of a play—an absolutely certain winner!—everybody says so! There's a definitely sure-fire scene where I pluck off my wedding ring—"The symbol of a lie!' I say, and throw it—"

"My sweet, I didn't bring you a birthday present because, four years ago, your birthday was on November the twentieth."

"I remember! A Saturday! With one of the very worst fogs, and we were both so depressed until we found it was my birthday. And then we had a gorgeous time and very nearly lived happily ever afterwards."

Hardelow winced, as he felt his normality slipping away.

"You little devil, darling—leave me alone now, can't you!"

He heard his own voice and thought it stagey, though he had spoken from his heart. Mabel was no actress but she had the disconcerting power of infecting others with her own theatricalism. He pulled himself together and blurted: "I'm fond of my wife and I intend to play straight with her."

"Those are the most beautiful words I've ever heard you say, Charlie!" The veiled contralto rippled down his spine: from a mist of dark copper the blue eyes adored him for his probity. In that moment he forgave himself for all his failures and saw himself as he wished to be. No one but Mabel could make him feel like that. It was wonderful and it was all damned nonsense which nevertheless contained a grain of truth about himself on which his pride could be nourished.

"Here comes one of the party—I'll tell you about the play later on—I know you'll jump at it. Oh, it's Frank Millard!"

"Broughby sent me on to chaperone you." Frank Millard, a member of the Stock Exchange, was lean and bony with large, dreamy eyes and a melodious voice.

"Frank, d'you know anything about that American Harold Crendon is bringing?" She added one of her innocent little lies that so often caused so much trouble. "He saw me on the floor at the Rialto and wanted to meet me. What's his name? Is he nice?"

"You mean, sweetheart, is he rich? I don't know. If he is, Crendon will have warned him about you—also, if he's poor."

"She wants to tell him about a play," chuckled Hardelow. He went out on to the deck and gazed down river, seeing nothing. That play!—she would infect him with the belief that it would be a genuine investment. He would, of course, lose more money over it than he could afford. Worse—the rush and scramble of it would keep him in touch with her—the very thing he did not want. He had built his life on the premise that, in any meaningful sense, he had forgotten her. He knew now that he had not forgotten her in any sense at all. He had been a fool to accept Broughby's invitation. If only he could think of some excuse for running home at once!

In the saloon, Mabel had removed the overall. Millard was telling himself that, though her colors did not match, the discords were resolved into an harmonious aura—or if it wasn't harmonious, it was certainly an aura. He produced a minute parcel.

"Happy birthday, Mabel!"

She scratched the wrapping from the jeweller's box and took out a gemmed brooch.

"Emeralds! Oh, Frank! That afternoon in Edinburgh!" She pinned the brooch on her green jumper—another color clash. "How dear of you to remember!"

"I've tried to forget!"

"To forget *me*, Frank?"

"I've tried to think of you as a girl I had a gorgeous time with—and it won't work. The girl turns back into you."

"But, dear, we finished and parted, liking each other better than ever."

"*You* had finished! And I thought I had."

"It will pass, Frank. Look at Charlie Hardelow. He's happily married. And I like to think he learned a tiny bit from me that helps him to be a good husband."

"I know you think that way—that's what does the damage. I shall never be happily married. Dammit, there is a girl I want to marry! I keep not-asking her, because I daren't think what I would do if you were to ask me to start again."

"I never would do a beastly thing like that!"

"I know. But it doesn't prevent me from imagining that you might—from hoping that you will."

"But, dear boy, I've told you!"

"You've told me that you don't want a repetition. Nor do I. Last time, we were hectic—we snatched excitedly at a passing happiness. You're doing it again now, with Broughby. It can't last. You don't really like this restless, happy-go-lucky existence. There's more genuine freedom in the suburbs than in bohemia—and we both know it. I could make a marriage settlement—"

From the deck came a whoop from Hardelow, then footsteps on the landing stage. Broughby was returning, accompanied by Crendon and his American friend.

As the American came into her line of vision, Mabel caught her breath. Of all the millions and millions of men in America it had to be this one! But, of course, he had contrived the meeting—might well have come to England for the purpose.

"Mabel, meet Mr. Stranack—Miss Rouse."

He had not changed in six years, she thought. He must be nearly forty now, but he was as springy as ever and his face still looked as if the skin had been stretched over it. He even seemed to have grown; but that was only because he was bigger than Broughby, who was bigger than the others. Alone of the party he was wearing a lounge suit, which fitted him so well that he managed to look as informal as everybody else.

She was steady as a rock through those first exchanges. He wished to be treated as a stranger—or perhaps he was waiting for her to take the first step. Perhaps he was merely anxious not to spoil the party. She might have guessed that he would never make a scene. Anyhow, he meant to give her a breathing space, which was something to be thankful for.

Broughby took Stranack off to show him over the launch. Millard joined Hardelow on deck, leaving Crendon to pay his respects to Mabel.

Harold Crendon was a barrister. After dawdling for three or four years in the criminal courts he had emerged as the best junior counsel for insurance litigation. In his middle thirties, he was already wondering whether it would pay him to take silk. Of middle size, he had broad shoulders and a broad face with a large nose and prominent chin. His personality had been attuned by nature to a law court: elsewhere, it gave the impression of being overgrown, as if the man himself could think only in superlatives.

He bore down upon Mabel, took her by the hand and snapped a diamond bracelet on her wrist.

"I ordered it for you two years ago, but you walked out on me before it was delivered."

"Harold!" The veiled contralto registered pain. Tears had come into her eyes. Such was her power of concentrating on the emotion of the moment that the whole problem of Broughby and Stranack shrank into the background. "I walked out because I thought you were tiring of me."

"What utter rot!"

"Yes!" She was looking at the bracelet as if it had betrayed her. She had been moved by this man as by no other and was again feeling the magnetism of him. "This very minute you've made me understand. I didn't know it was rot at the time."

"I have to point out that you soon consoled yourself?"

"Very soon! There was hardly six months of real misery."

His self-assurance was unshaken. To gain time he blustered.

"Will you have the goodness to sit down and give me your whole attention!"

"I can't sit down—I've things to do. And there's nothing for either of us to say. I couldn't mope for the rest of my life. So why not George Broughby? He's a dear and I'm fond of him. But I can't go on with it, now!"

Harold glowered at her. She dropped onto a settee as if he had flung her there.

"You little fool—it's all too late!" he said, with anger. "I've just got engaged to be married."

"Then you have lost nothing. I'm glad!" She added: "I hope your fiancée knows she's lucky."

He stood over her, pointing at her.

"I believed, however mistakenly, that you had walked out on me. Those were the very words I used just now. Why did you correct me?" He went on: "You had no right to tell me the truth. You're selfish, mean and cruel. So am I, I suppose. You have all my weaknesses and most of my vices, and if I had any sense I'd be thankful to you for letting go. As it is—"

"*Sh!* Don't get so worked up, darling. You'll be able to forget when you start a new life with her. Thank you ever so much for this lovely bracelet!"

"Shut up! I feel it would not be fair to my fiancée to go on with our engagement. That's easily said, but it settles nothing. We have to find a way out of this tragic muddle in which you have landed us—and at present I can see no way."

There sounded the whirr of the starter, then the low purr of the engine ticking over.

Broughby came into the cabin.

"I say, Crendon, will you take us as far as the pool so that I can help Mabel get things started?" As Crendon assented and moved to the door: "And thanks for bringing Stranack. He's an asset!"

Mabel sensed that Broughby had something on his mind, and remembered uneasily that he had been alone with Stranack.

"Stranack is the right sort," he said, lowering his voice. "But, being American, he may be strange to some of our little ways—meaning your little ways, darling. So be careful not to give him a wrong impression."

"What's the right impression, George?"

"That you and I—"

"But you promised me that we'd say nothing about us today!"

"That you and I might be considering the idea of getting married. Put that truth over in a form which he will accept. A little unconventionality won't hurt, but—you know exactly what I mean, Mabel!"

He was warning her not to make a blue joke in the presence of Arthur Stranack. That was funny, she thought, and she laughed a little, but without enjoyment because she was becoming nervous. The throb of the engines quickened. The launch had put off with its party of six intelligent, law-abiding persons.

# Chapter Three

Things, thought Mabel, could take a shape of their own sometimes as if they were trying to warn you, though you couldn't do anything about it. She had the eerie feeling that all the events of the last six years were running up behind her and when they reached her they would explode. George asking her to marry him at the very moment when Arthur Stranack popped up *meant* something.

Then, too, Harold Crendon had behaved very strangely, talking about breaking off his engagement. Being a professional talker, he always made everything seem so urgent. The other two didn't matter so much. Charlie Hardelow often got excited about nothing and Frank rather liked having something to be sad about.

The eeriness faded while she was loading the tray. After all, what was she afraid of? That somebody might make a fuss and embarrass the others? Or that five of her friends might become five enemies?

As she approached the companionway to the deck, she felt stage-fright. The tray was very heavy—she doubted whether she could carry it in one hand.

"Allow me, Miss Rouse."

"Thank you, Mr. Stranack. It's heavier than I thought."

In his glance was neither threat nor promise. Why, she wondered, had he contrived this meeting?

At the Tower of London, Broughby took the wheel from Crendon. Mr. Stranack remarked to Miss Rouse that it was a grand old pile, and Miss Rouse made the trite answer. The other men noted that Mabel was behaving nicely, that the American was not englamoured—which they thought a very satisfactory circumstance for all concerned.

Crendon, joining the party on deck, contrived to corner Mabel.

"I may as well tell you I've got an idea." He spoke as if he were still angry with her. "I haven't worked out the details—but still, it's an idea. I'll tell you about it later."

Crendon, she told herself, would be the flash point for the explosion. But what explosion? As she could not marry Broughby, she would have to leave him tomorrow. What harm could there be in Crendon making plans? It was the eerie feeling again—but she had often had that sort of feeling without anything dire happening.

Ignoring the growing heat of the day, she flitted restlessly from deck to saloon and back again. While they were passing through the Port of London the men chattered to each other about the shipping—all a little too polite, she thought. Below Tilbury, Hardelow took his turn at the wheel. When Broughby came on deck, Mabel handed him a cocktail. His eyes asked her why the party was hanging fire.

Mabel was fast losing her head. As usual on these occasions her thoughts retreated into fantasy. Suppose Arthur Stranack were to fall overboard? Everything would then be so much simpler. What an awful thought! Arthur was the kindest man on earth—and besides, he was a strong swimmer. Then suppose they all had a frightful quarrel, with guns and things! But again that wouldn't be any good unless poor Arthur were killed, which would be horribly unfair. The real troublemaker was Harold Crendon, but it really wouldn't help much if he—

She jerked herself back to reality. At least, there was no need to go on wondering what Arthur Stranack meant to do. She caught his eye, held it, then glanced significantly below. Presently he went below. Within a minute, she picked up a tray and followed.

He was lounging on the farther settee and did not rise until she had come close.

"Are you happy, Mabel? If the answer is 'yes', I'll fade out."

All shyness of him left her. She answered with a spontaneity she had not intended.

"I don't know. I suppose I am. Anyway, it doesn't matter. Why didn't you divorce me before I left the States?"

"I told you I would divorce you the moment you asked me, but not before. Why didn't you ask me?"

"I don't know."

"I do, Mabel. And it's all come true. I *have* sought you out. And now I'm going to say it—and mean it. Ready? I'm sorry for my fifty per cent share in wrecking our marriage. In six years, I've learnt how not to make some of those mistakes. I want you to come back to me. Clean slate for both of us!"

He certainly was the kindest man on earth—she had been hoping he would be unkind. It would have been easier in the end.

"Now you've made me utterly miserable!" She saw now that she had wasted six years and spoilt herself for him, out of pique. "It wouldn't work, Arthur. All you know about me is that I've been what is commonly called unfaithful to you, and you're willing to forget it. There are rotten streaks in me you know nothing about. I accept jewelry!" She flashed Crendon's bracelet against Millard's brooch. "And money, too! In a way, I loot my friends."

"You didn't loot me. You knew I had a hundred thousand dollars in gilt edged. It's still there. If there's any of it left when we've paid those men back, you can wangle it from me." He added: "Just now, I'm in the diplomatic service, but I can stage a transfer if you don't feel you could manage that sort of life, just yet."

"I'm trying to be sensible and you won't let me!" For a second or less, she wavered. "It's no good, Arthur. You're forgiving and kind and gentle and insanely generous—and I couldn't live up to it. You would keep your part of the bargain, but I don't trust myself to keep mine. I'd hurt you all over again—and hate myself for being so mean."

He made no answer, looked as if he were paying no heed. She went on:

"Divorce me, and have done with it. But not with Broughby—he's standing for Parliament. I'll sign a confession. It'll be done in America, of course. And over here no one need know that we have been married. I mean—in a way—we're both free."

Mabel's appeal lay in her intuitive flashes, which owed nothing to conscious thought. When she reasoned aloud her vitality was blanketed under layers of muddled banalities.

Stranack waited while she talked and repeated herself. When he spoke, he made no reference to her words.

"Think it over, Mabel." His voice was gentle beyond bearing.

To escape from him, she hurried back to the deck. He followed her closely. They were just in time to see a sailing yacht run across the fairway of the motor boat. The boat rolled as Hardelow brought the wheel over. Stranack caught Mabel and steadied her. He was still holding her when the bow struck the soft mud of the Essex bank. At the impact they swayed, then steadied. As if they were alone together, Mabel stood on tip-toe and pressed her mouth to his.

"God, I wish I hadn't done that!" she gasped. "You see how rotten I am, Arthur—I meant not to!"

Broughby took control. Hardelow, running about in search of a sympathetic audience, fixed on Mabel. As a matter of routine, the dinghy was lowered and Crendon got in it, pottered round the bow and confirmed the obvious. Everybody went aft, for counterpoise, while Broughby tried to pull clear by reversing. But the bow was firmly wedged. A dozen feet from the bow the mud sloped upwards from the water to the verge of the marshland. When it was certain that the boat was undamaged, Broughby summed up.

"We could signal for a tug, but it might be the devil of a time, to say nothing of the hullabaloo, before we get one." He flourished a tide table. "If we stay put, the incoming tide should float us off in two and a half hours. What does everybody think?"

"Lunch! As soon as I've got over the shock," said Mabel, helping herself to a second gin of generous proportions.

# Chapter Four

The lunch began very well. The mishap to the boat had broken the reserve which had threatened to freeze the party. Everybody did something and everything turned out to be rather amusing, even locking the little tables together to make a big table and unpacking the caterer's basket.

The first hitch came with the cold chicken.

"George! Those wretched people haven't carved the fowls. I can't carve and you aren't really any good at it. Harold, you look as if you could carve!"

"I know I do—and it's given me a complex."

"Why not take a chance on me!" offered Stranack. "I wasted two years on a medical course in the belief that I was meant to be a surgeon."

"How tactful of you!" said Mabel. "George, give him your chair. Oh, but we haven't a carving knife!"

"I can scare up something that'll do," said Broughby and went out.

"It hurts to hear that you can't carve, Mabel," said Hardelow. "I believed you had all the domestic accomplishments and virtues."

"I might have a dab at the accomplishments," returned Mabel, "but the rest of it sounds much too difficult."

Crendon sniggered. Millard scowled at Hardelow. Mabel—he told himself—never said that kind of thing unless some lout goaded her to a retort.

Broughby returned and handed Stranack an ugly looking instrument. It was a short butcher's knife. It had a black wooden handle and a broad based blade. The blade tapered to a point, so that it had the shape of a right-angled triangle.

"This is better than a fancy carver!" said Stranack as he used it with a deftness which inspired Mabel to lyrical enthusiasm—a state from which she did not depart. She became noisy, and the party liked it—joyous nonsense put over with a vitality that evoked willing response.

She was, in fact, too successful too early in the lunch. When spontaneity flagged, she made more intensive efforts. Jollity slipped away and thought was creeping in. Again and again her eyes rested on Stranack. By that impulsive kiss on deck, she had further confused her values. The eerie feeling was coming back and she sought refuge in boisterousness.

One of her jokes approached the limit, and one overstepped it. The men, except Broughby, cackled politely, but their faces had lengthened. So far, nothing had happened which could not be forgotten, but they had a lively fear that she might produce a moment of acute embarrassment. Each man secretly blamed one of the others for egging her on—then thought uneasily of his own feelings for her.

Stranack was hearing the echo of her words of an hour ago: *'It wouldn't work, Arthur.'* Millard was glad she had refused his offer to settle down with him in the suburbs. Crendon's eye was caught by the bracelet flashing on her wrist: He wished he had not been so definite about breaking off his engagement: Mabel might think he meant to marry her. Broughby was thinking of his Parliamentary career, thankful that no announcement had been made to the others.

Crendon alone made an attempt to come to her rescue.

"Silence everybody!" he shouted with mock solemnity. "It's Mabel's birthday. I've prepared a nice little speech about her and I intend to deliver it."

"Keep it clean!" chirped Mabel.

"'Keep it clean,'" parried Crendon, "*is* the slogan which this gallant lady adopted when she decided to become a professional entertainer. As 'Cherry Dane' she wins admiration for her gracefulness and her beauty. She plays for the hearty and wholesome laugh—she does not play for the facile guffaw. On the threshold of her career in the theatre, the one thing she asks—the one thing she is determined to have—is—"

"*Marriage!*" ejaculated Mabel.

The moment of acute embarrassment had come. In the silence, she added: "That was what you meant, wasn't it, Harold?"

The ambiguity of her words, which might have applied to his own intentions, disconcerted Crendon. Hardelow, the least affected, jumped in.

"He thinks you're proposing to him, my dear. Mind he doesn't say 'yes' and make himself the happiest man on earth."

"Charlie! I'd forgotten my promise to you about that play. Let's tell them about it, now that Harold has finished his speech. And a very nice speech too, only he ought to have stood up."

As she attempted to rise, one leg of her chair fouled a socket in the floor. Frank Millard, unaware of this, took a firm grip, intending only to steady her. But Mabel thought he was trying to prevent her from standing up.

"Don't!" she cried. "Surely I can say a few words to the company on my own birthday!" She made a scuffle of it. By ill-luck the bracelet Crendon had given her scraped the back of Millard's hand.

"Frank—I'm terribly sorry! Oh, it's bleeding—mind your trousers! Quick, George—the First Aid box!"

"The patient is expected to recover," said Millard. "It's all right, dear—it'll stop bleeding in a minute. My fault entirely!"

Mabel couldn't leave it at that. She elaborated her apology: she crooned over the trifling injury: she skidded into sheer silliness.

Broughby took her by the elbows, marched her across the saloon and carried her up the companionway. By the wheelhouse he set her on her feet and opened the door of the corridor.

"George, dear, I'm not drunk, if that's in your mind."

"It's in my mind that you've forgotten what I told you about behaving yourself in front of Stranack."

She laughed loudly. He shuffled her down the corridor and opened the door of her cabin.

"I warned you I wasn't a fit wife for a rising politician."

"And I was fool enough to contradict you!"

So she need not bother any more about how to marry George Broughby, decided Mabel.

"You weren't a fool, George, dear. I thought it a perfectly charming way of saying goodbye."

Broughby weakened. He was angry and disgusted with her, and a moment ago had hoped he would never see her after tomorrow. She would not cling, nor wait to be paid off, like some others. She would blow him a kiss and dance out of his life, leaving behind her a fragrance that would linger for years and smother memory of her witless vulgarities.

In the saloon Stranack was bandaging Millard's hand. Hardelow affected to be reading a book on economics. Crendon was sprawling on a settee contemplating his shoes. The party had disintegrated. If the guests had been able to do so they would have made excuses to leave.

Broughby had brought the crockery basket with him. When the others perceived its purpose they were excessively anxious to help. The dining table was reduced to its component parts.

Broughby picked up the crockery basket, carried it back to the galley for the eventual attention of the contractor's staff. The butcher's knife, because it had to be handled gingerly, had been dealt with last—so remained at the top ready to the hand of anyone who might glance into the galley on his way down the passage.

In the corridor he hesitated. He had been needlessly offensive to Mabel. Might make some kind of apology. Fathead! he warned himself. She is willing to fade out. Leave well alone. At best she would be a handicap.

Intending to go back to the saloon, he nevertheless turned round and knocked on Mabel's door, which was shut.

"Got everything you want?"

"Yes, thanks. I'll be quite rested by tea time."

From her voice he judged that she was standing close to the door. She ought to be lying down, by now. Hell! Concentrate on the bye-election and forget her.

Before returning to the saloon he went on deck to take

observations, which revealed nothing new. Going below, he found Stranack hovering by the wheelhouse.

"I've forgotten where I go for a wash."

"Through that door, down the corridor, last door on the right."

Stranack entered the corridor, shutting the door behind him. When he had taken a few steps, he had an oblique view of orange satin and a bare arm—for Mabel's door was now open.

He would have continued on his way if he had been permitted.

"Arthur!"

As their eyes met, she smiled. She was lying on the coverlet, propped on one arm.

"I ought to have shut the door, but it's so hot—I forgot everybody would be going past." She was flushed and more than a little bedraggled. One shoulder strap had slipped. Her skirt lay on the floor, beside it her jumper, with the brooch still pinned to it. On the bed, out of her line of vision, was a shoe. There was a gash in one of her stockings.

"D'you want me to shut the door?"

Waiting for her answer, he let his eye travel from her chin to her throat, her shoulders, and come to rest on the diamond bracelet.

"Crendon gave it to me." She unclipped it and thrust it under the pillows. "I'll give it back to him at the very first chance I get—I'll give back all my jewelry."

"Why?"

His voice was cold and his eyes showed disillusion. Mabel ignored the warning.

"Arthur!" She rolled his name on her tongue. "I talked a lot of nonsense this morning. Your offer took me by surprise and I wanted to run away and think. But on deck—when I felt your arm round me—I knew I must come back. I'll leave Broughby as soon as we get off this boat."

She 'plucked' the wedding ring from her finger, held it as if to let an audience have a good look at it.

"'The symbol of a lie!'" She flung it across the cabin. "I have the real one locked away—the one you gave me, Arthur."

It was characteristic of poor Mabel that she had to tell the truth that was in her by means of a ham performance, gagged from a bad scene in a poor play, which would have cost Charles Hardelow more than he could afford—if it had ever been put on the stage.

The *Astarte* remained aground for some forty minutes after Stranack had rejoined the others in the saloon.

# Chapter Five

At Westminster Pier, the still air magnified the vibrations of Big Ben booming half past five. Broughby left the wheelhouse as Inspector Kyle stepped aboard, followed by Sergeant Dobson. The two plainclothes men remained on the pier, mounting guard on the *Astarte* so unobtrusively that the passers by on the Embankment were unaware that police were taking action.

"Your note says that murder has been committed on this launch, Mr. Broughby?" Kyle spoke as if he thought there might have been some mistake.

"Correct!" Broughby led them into the corridor, past the galley to the cabin that had been Mabel's.

"Behind that door," he said and pointed to a narrow strip of paper secured at each end with a postage stamp. "That's the best I could do for a seal—the signature is mine."

"Then, there are some other people on this boat?"

"Four men. They're in the saloon. I thought you'd want to come here first." He produced a key. "My fingerprints will be on the handle and all over the door. Shall I open it?"

"I'll do that," said Kyle. The sergeant handed him a folded silk handkerchief.

"Press the lever and slide the door to your left."

On the bed, Kyle saw the body of a woman in orange satin under-clothes. The head, throat and part of the chest were covered with a green jumper, bloodstained. From the green jumper protruded the black handle of a knife of which the blade was, by inference, sunk in the throat.

Court histories and political biographies record that more than one of the women like Mabel have met violent death in just such an impromptu manner. That green jumper had been used solely because it happened to be to hand. The emerald brooch, which Millard had given her, dangled on a loosened strand. One shoe was still on the bed. The tartan skirt lay on the floor where she herself had let it fall.

Kyle's eye travelled to the bare arms above the head, noted that the fingers were ringless: it roamed slowly round the cabin, then returned to the black handle of the knife. It was obviously of a kind that could be bought at any ironmonger's.

"D'you know anything about that knife, Mr. Broughby?"

From where Broughby was standing he could not see into the cabin. He did not move. He did not want to see that cabin ever again.

"The knife is part of the galley equipment, though we used it today in the saloon." He explained that it had been placed in the basket on top of the unwashed crockery. "Anyone who happened to glance into the galley could have seen that knife."

Kyle noted the answer but made no comment. Presently he asked:

"You know who deceased is, of course?"

"Mabel Rouse—professional name 'Cherry Dane.'" He gave an address and added: "She appeared in floor shows and bit parts. I can tell you a good deal about her when you're ready for it."

Kyle glanced again at the ringless fingers.

"Was she married or single?"

"Single. At least I have strong reason for believing so. If she has ever been married, she must have had a divorce." He added: "She said she was twenty-eight—which was about right. I'd better mention that I was running a flat for her—the address I gave you. I bought her that wedding ring."

Kyle studied the fingers a third time and for the third time observed that they were ringless. Too soon to go into that.

"Can you give me some idea how it happened, Mr. Broughby?"

"Yes, but we must have the others in on that. Will you come and meet them?" He added: "We intended to run down the river to Southend regatta." He reported the mishap.

Kyle turned to Sergeant Dobson.

"Take charge here. The team will be along in a couple of minutes. I shall be in the saloon."

Following Broughby, Kyle stopped by the wheelhouse and beckoned to the nearer of the two plain clothes men.

"No one is to leave the launch until I pass him out."

Broughby opened doors disclosing the companionway leading down to the saloon.

"Here is Detective Inspector Kyle."

The four men rose, not indeed as one man but as four highly individualized persons. They had the air of men who had suffered sudden bereavement, to which was added the slightly smug expression which commonly settles upon the innocent when under police scrutiny.

Broughby introduced them, adding information deemed to be of interest to the police.

"Mr. Harold Crendon, barrister-at-law, Western Circuit, chambers in Lincoln's Inn: Mr. Frank Millard, member of the Stock Exchange, Millard and Bush, Copthall Avenue: Mr. Charles Hardelow, chartered accountant, partner in his father's firm in Victoria Street: Mr. Stranack—" Broughby hesitated. "I'm afraid I don't know anything about Mr. Stranack except that he is a friend of Crendon's, and that he's a citizen of the United States."

"He's in the diplomatic service," supplied Crendon. "Quartered at the Embassy."

"As I'm a foreigner, Inspector, you'll want to see my papers." Stranack drew from his breast pocket that which looked like an ordinary passport, but was not. Kyle scanned it, checked the photograph with the original and handed it back.

"Mr. Stranack, I have to detain everybody here for questioning. If you wish to claim diplomatic immunity—"

"I wish to claim nothing, Inspector," said the American. "You may take it that I shall not communicate with the Embassy until you've finished with me."

"Thank you, Mr. Stranack." There was a pause. Kyle was waiting for Broughby. He glanced round the saloon, becoming aware of its size—it would hold thirty guests without squashing.

"Well, gentlemen, I'm waiting for one of you to tell me what happened and how the killer managed to get away from the five of you."

Another long silence followed, in which he had the impression that each was waiting for another to speak.

"He hasn't got away," said Broughby. "He's here—one of us in this saloon killed her. We don't know which one.

"One of us!" he repeated. "And theoretically that includes me."

Kyle looked from one face to another, learning nothing except that they would be a difficult bunch to handle. Whether it was a put-up job or not, they had taken a considered position and were standing together. Routine provided for this tactic—nail them down in their position before breaking them individually.

Broughby spoke again.

"If you're ready to hear the circumstances—"

"Before we go into details," interrupted Kyle, "I'd like to know whether you all agree with what Mr. Broughby has said—that one of you in this room killed that girl?"

He happened to glance at Stranack.

"I agree that it is an inescapable inference!" said Stranack.

Millard and Hardelow signified agreement. Crendon made a qualification.

"Broughby's statement is true, but misleading on one point. He intended to convey to you our belief that one of *four* of us in this room—Broughby, Hardelow, Millard or myself—killed Mabel Rouse. Not one of the four of us suspects Mr. Stranack."

There were murmurs of assent. Crendon went on:

"With that amendment, I accept Broughby's statement. I can add—in the hope that it will help you—that I personally am convinced that Hardelow can also be eliminated. And I shall be happy to give evidence to that effect at the proper time."

Kyle was delighted. By inference Crendon accused Broughby and Millard jointly or severally. If the others would follow suit, there would be hope of the familiar situation in which conspirators fall out and accuse each other.

"I can't eliminate anybody—except Stranack, of course," said Broughby.

"I agree with Crendon," put in Millard. "Stranack is out of it. I blot out Hardelow as well. He hasn't been out of my sight long enough."

There came a moan from Hardelow.

"That puts me in a very humiliating position. I ought to return the compliment, but I can't eliminate anybody—except Stranack, of course."

Kyle was disappointed. One more try.

"Can you eliminate anybody, Mr. Stranack?"

"Sorry, Inspector. I didn't keep tab on people's movements."

Kyle refused to give up hope. If he could split them at only one point at the start, a mass of detailed work would be by-passed.

"Then we come back to Mr. Broughby's statement. You all agree on eliminating Mr. Stranack. Two of you also eliminate Mr. Hardelow. That means—letting me off the 'misters,' please—Millard suspects Crendon and Broughby. Crendon suspects Millard and—"

"Pardon *me*, Inspector! I suspect no one. I have not a tittle of evidence against anybody. You may reasonably believe or disbelieve my statements. You may draw the inference that either Broughby or Millard must be guilty. But you cannot attribute to me a suspicion of either, nor of both."

A lawyer's distinction, thought Kyle, but could find no answer. In general terms, he disliked lawyers. This one evidently intended to throw his weight about.

"Quite right, Mr. Crendon, I apologize. The fact is, I have never before handled a case involving gentlemen of your position." He was being spuriously humble about it. "But when we get down to bedrock, I'm on familiar ground, as you might say. Crooks generally accuse one another—and that puts 'em where we want 'em. You gentlemen have dug your toes in and are telling me that not one of you has so much as a suspicion of any one of the others—which is much the same thing, only—gentlemanly side up, if you understand me."

He paused, confident of getting his effect.

"Do you realize that it's possible—I only say possible—that you might all be charged with murder?"

"Of course we do!" exploded Hardelow. "That's why we're behaving like this. For God's sake, Inspector, don't get it into your head that we're a bunch of gangsters trying to pull a fast one on the police!"

Kyle, looking at the round, earnest face, suppressed a smile. "Gangsters were not in my mind."

"If you suspect this is a criminal conspiracy," cut in Millard, "ask yourself why we didn't dump poor Mabel overboard. At worst, it would have been much safer than voluntarily walking into the lion's den like this."

Before Kyle could prevent it, Crendon had seized the initiative.

"There can be no charge of conspiracy!"

Kyle sniffed as if he had received a blow in the face.

"Do you believe, Inspector, that—within the confines of *this launch*—it would be possible to plan and carry out a murder—and agree upon a course of action to be taken in regard to the police—unless Mr. Stranack were one of the conspirators? You do not!"

Kyle was ready to climb down rather than attack Stranack, who could remove himself as a witness if he were offended.

"Evidence will be adduced," continued Crendon, "that I met Mr. Stranack in Washington last year when I was there for a fortnight on Government business. He landed in England for the first time five weeks ago and looked me up yesterday. He mentioned that he had seen 'Miss Cherry Dane' doing her floor show and would like to meet her. I telephoned Broughby and fixed it. No one will believe that Mr. Stranack would bring scandal on his Embassy—to say nothing of risking his neck—in order to oblige four men, three of whom he had never met until this morning."

Another lawyer's point, noted Kyle. It was common knowledge that when all the conspirators were arrested one of them generally squealed. Who but a lawyer would have spotted that Stranack's presence could be used to rob the police of a powerful weapon?

"*Furthermore,*" resumed Crendon, "I ask you to remember that each of us has a career. At the trial—and we devoutly hope that you will be able to bring this case to trial—a single adverse comment by the judge on the conduct of any one of us would take years to live down. Of the five of us present, four will be desperately anxious to help you find the murderer."

So far, Kyle admitted to himself, his shock tactics had yielded nothing. It was a novelty to him to be bullied by the suspects in a murder case. Their unusual behavior, however, did not mean that they were unusual men. Broughby, he had looked up. Crendon's name was often cropping up in the papers as counsel in insurance litigation. The other two were of the same social stratum. No matter! The job would be the same, even if it had to be done with kid gloves.

"I say everybody!" It was a joyous shout from Hardelow. "Why are we all harping on murder? We told the Inspector it was murder, but we may be wrong. Suppose it was suicide?"

Kyle alone was startled. He had made a recruit's mistake in accepting the statement of murder without proof. He had let the special circumstances disturb his routine. It was Broughby who unconsciously saved the detective's face.

"Rot! Mabel would never commit suicide."

"Presumably," said Crendon, "we shall now adjourn to Scotland Yard for questioning?"

Kyle had had enough of Crendon for the present.

"We'll see what we can do on the spot, first," he said. "You are anxious to cooperate—four of you, anyhow. I will therefore ask you all to remain in this saloon until I come back—and in the meantime to give my staff any help they may require."

They would wait long enough, reflected Kyle, to get over their enthusiasm for presenting neat little riddles in law to the police. Crendon, for instance, was going to be taught that there's quite a lot of law that never crops up in a law court.

# Chapter Six

Sergeant Dobson met Kyle at the head of the companionway.

"River police launch standing by, sir. I told 'em they'd have to cruise 'emselves off till the doctor and the photographers have finished. Dr. Maenton waiting for you now."

Kyle closed the doors of the saloon behind him.

"There are five men in there, Dobson—one of 'em a lawyer. You heard me—a lawyer! They've promised not to move until I come back." He grinned. "They don't know how long I'm going to be—the lawyer can work that out for 'em! Send a man in to take their dabs. One of 'em—Millard—has a blood stain on his trousers, but he's got a bandage on his hand, so he'll have a tale. We'll have the blood group of that stain right away. They're to be treated very lightly—they're all smiles and we want 'em like that."

The conference with Dr. Maenton took place behind the closed door of the forward guest cabin. He was an able but gloomy little man. In their work together, Kyle had picked up a little physiology and Maenton had picked up a lot of cautiousness.

"I haven't much for you," said Maenton. "She has been dead for about three hours." He inclined to leave it at that.

"Would it be going too far to say that the knife sticking in her throat might have something to do with it?" prompted Kyle.

"We need look no further for the originating cause," pronounced Maenton. "Judging by the position of the arms and the limited ejection of blood I think it's a fairly safe guess that the examination will determine the cause of death as shock following partial asphyxia."

"Very interesting!" remarked Kyle politely. "Did she do all that by herself, or did somebody help her?"

Kyle had expected a confident assurance. But the doctor looked gloomier than ever.

"You don't want me to comment on the position of that jumper which, of course, would have unsighted her. Nor is it my province to dwell upon the psychological absurdity of suicide in such circumstances."

"Try this one, Doctor. If she did stab herself, could she have wiped the handle of the knife afterwards?"

"No—no! That would have been definitely impossible."

"In your opinion, how long could she have lived after the blow had been delivered?"

"In my opinion—based on a cursory examination and subject to correction at the post mortem examination—a few seconds."

When the doctor had gone, Kyle stepped across the corridor to deceased's cabin.

Sergeant Dobson was standing in the doorway.

"I'd like you to look at that skirt, sir."

Kyle knelt and peered at the tartan skirt lying close to the bed.

"Looks like the imprint of a shoe, ball to toe, left side of left shoe—that's what I see."

"So do I, sir. It isn't the doctor's shoe. I warned him, and I watched him until he'd finished." He added: "Simpkins said he doubted whether the photo would be any use—couldn't get a shadow on it as it lay."

"The lab can have a look at that. See to the packing yourself, will you. Ask 'em to make a rush job of it. Collect all the shoes you want off the gentry-an'-aristocracy in the saloon. But leave Stranack out of it. He has diplomatic immunity—he's waiving it at present, but he might change his mind. Treat him like glass, but you needn't be afraid of that lawyer. *Hi*, what's that?"

Kyle was looking at a broad white circle chalked on the carpet in a corner of the cabin.

"That's where I found a wedding ring, sir. It's packed now and in the inventory."

Kyle nodded. He remembered that Broughby had spoken as if there had been a wedding ring on the dead girl's finger. While he continued his scrutiny of the cabin, his thoughts played round that wedding ring. Something funny there! Women don't drop wedding rings by accident. Before taking an afternoon nap, a woman decides to put her wedding ring on the floor in a corner of the cabin. Ridiculous!

'The wrong shows the right.' That slogan had helped him more than once. No one had 'put' the wedding ring on the carpet. If she had taken it off before lying down, she'd have put it on the dressing-table; and if it had been brushed off by accident it couldn't have rolled some ten feet along a carpet. Therefore the ring had been thrown to the corner of the cabin.

Assume murder. The murderer removes the ring and flings it into the corner of the cabin. Physically possible—but too darned silly to have happened.

Therefore the girl herself flung it there. While she was lying on the bed. In what circumstances does a woman take off her wedding ring and fling it across the room? When she's having a hell of a dust-up with her old man—even if he's only an honorary old man, as you might say.

But Broughby, innocent or guilty, would not have said it was on her finger if he knew it was on the floor, where the police would be sure to find it.

Therefore she was not having a hammer-an'-tongs with Broughby when she threw off the ring. Having a hammer-an'-tongs with somebody else? Then why did she feature the wedding ring?

"Shows it's no good guessing without the facts!" he muttered, and left the cabin. In the corridor he caught sight of one of his own men apparently looting the wardrobe in the forward guest cabin.

"What the devil are you up to, Bissett?"

"Looking for trousers, sir, at owner's request. That blood stain. Millard said he must be provided with another pair or he couldn't cooperate."

By the wheelhouse Kyle found Sergeant Dobson arguing with a member of the river police.

"All right, sergeant. They can move the body as soon as you've packed that skirt and finished the inventory. I shall be in my room. Leave one man on board and two on the pier."

The doors of the saloon were opened with some violence and Crendon appeared.

"I take it, Inspector, that your investigations will not be impeded if we have these doors open? It's very hot in the saloon."

"That's all right, Mr. Crendon."

Before stepping ashore, Kyle spoke under his breath to Dobson.

"Tough on him! He hoped I'd object, so's he could trot up an Act o' Parliament about it."

Bissett passed by, carrying a pair of white flannel trousers.

# Chapter Seven

The white trousers, which were too long for Millard, increased the effect of lopsidedness caused by wearing one shoe. The three others who were also partly shoeless became aware that the American alone looked as unruffled as when he had come aboard. The company itself was becoming lopsided.

Millard drew back the curtain of a porthole and looked over the pier to the Embankment.

"No reporters in sight. So far, we haven't drawn a crowd."

No one accepted the opening for a little light chatter to ease the burden of silence. Their social instincts were paralyzed. In the mind of the innocent was the knowledge that a man of their own kind, sharing their ethical outlook, had stepped beyond the pale by committing murder. Not yet could four out of the five imagine themselves in personal danger of conviction.

In addition they were suffering the emotional confusion of hating the man who had killed Mabel without having anything approaching a reasonable suspicion of which particular man was to be hated.

"I can't stand a lot of this waiting about!" whined Hardelow. He wanted to talk and listen to others talking. His amiability had already converted the murderer into an abstraction which could be mentioned without hurting anybody's feelings. "Now that we have reported to the police, I don't see why we have to go on staring in front of us like stuffed sheep."

Stranack answered, with the air of a man rising to a difficult occasion.

"I don't know anything about police procedure in this country, but I guess Crendon's advice not to discuss the case would hold good anywhere. Once you start discussion you agree upon a version. The police drill a hole in it, and there you are."

"And if we don't agree to a version, we shall contradict each other," objected Hardelow. "And anyway, not one of us intends to tell the whole truth about poor Mabel."

"Not one of us knows it," said Millard. "We shall each tell a different truth about her. And we shall all be disbelieved."

"You needn't worry," Crendon assured him. "Discrepancy on small points makes a good impression. Anyway, you're out of it, Hardelow. Millard and I have both given you an alibi."

"But the police don't seem to have accepted it, or they wouldn't have taken my other shoe—though how you can leave a footprint on a boat on a dry day beats me!"

Broughby, who had been holding himself in a kind of special aloofness, now unbent.

"What we tell the police can't prove anything, or it would already have proved it to us."

"So unless they find fingerprints and cigarette ash in the right places, they'll never know for certain," said Millard.

"And the imaginary man knew they'd never know for certain!" cried Hardelow. "That's what he was building on. Doubt! And they'll have to give him the benefit of the doubt which he created himself."

"He isn't an imaginary man," snapped Crendon. "He's one of us."

"You know what I mean!" grumbled Hardelow. "He worked out that we couldn't all be charged together, himself included, owing to Stranack's presence—oh!—"

Hardelow broke off in pink confusion. Crendon laughed.

"You've just remembered that I brought Stranack to this party—if he'll ever forgive me!"

"I say, Crendon! Look here!" floundered Hardelow. "You don't for one moment think that I think—"

"Of course I don't! And you don't think I think etcetera—when I point out that this murder could not have occurred, in the manner in which it did occur, if you had not run the boat into the mud."

"Take-it-easy!" shouted Stranack.

Instead of resenting the peremptory order, all four took it in meek silence. In their eyes the American had become a superior being, standing outside their peril.

Stranack, who had no such view of himself, apologized to his host.

"Sorry, Broughby! But it did strike me that in a minute we should all be accusing each other."

"That's what we're doing already," returned Broughby. "I agree we'd better not do it out loud."

Silence was restored. While they waited for Inspector Kyle, the thoughts of the four innocent men hovered about Mabel Rouse until their hatred of the unknown fifth was fanned to murderous proportions.

# Chapter Eight

In this tidiest of murder hunts, the desk work gave extraordinarily little trouble to anybody. Within a couple of hours of leaving the *Astarte*, Kyle had before him all the real evidence he was likely to get.

The first report covered the fingerprints. As was already known, there were none on the handle of the knife, which had been wiped clean. On the door of deceased's cabin were two distinct prints only, one made by deceased and the other by Broughby. There were other prints too blurred for identification. On the wedding ring were blurred prints which could have been made by deceased and could not have been made by any of the men.

While the detailed report of the microscopic examination of the tartan skirt was being typed, Kyle had received a short summary on the house telephone.

"The outline was faint in parts and not continuous. We are satisfied that it could have been made by Specimen No. 3—which is Crendon's shoe—"

"Good!" said Kyle. "That fits in nicely."

"I said could have been made, Inspector. We cannot assert that it was made by that shoe and none other. It could have been made by Specimen No. 2—Millard's shoe—or any other shoe of the same size, making the same deposits. Specimens 1 and 4 are excluded by size."

"That's what I call a yes-and-no answer," grumbled Kyle and added to himself: "unless we can get a dovetail on Crendon."

Sergeant Dobson came in with the inventory.

"Dobson, if one of those men on that boat killed that girl, he did it for love, or jealousy."

"What price blackmail?"

"Or blackmail. He comes in with the knife in his hand to settle her threats once for all—and she throws off her wedding ring."

"What for, sir?"

"Exactly! Or a lover comes in to ask her to leave Broughby and come to him. She says 'okay,' throws off Broughby's ring—and he doesn't bump her off. Or she tells him to go to hell and she doesn't take off the wedding ring." As the other looked blank, Kyle added: "Or it might be a jealousy-merchant—you get the same thing. There's no point at which she throws off the wedding ring and then gets bumped off."

"I'm getting it, sir. She throw the ring at the killer?"

"Anyway, she threw it—and I'm trying to catch it," said Kyle, without conviction. "We shan't want those shoes—send 'em back and say I shan't be long. Let's have a look at that inventory. Did you find anything in the bed after they'd moved her?"

"Only the bedclothes. Do I go over the road with you, sir?"

"No. I'll send word if I want you. I'll take Carfax—his shorthand is the best."

It was nearly nine when Kyle reached the pier. The loungers on the Embankment had thinned out and the pier was deserted except for the two plain clothes men.

He was at his most urbane when he stepped aboard and descended to the saloon—the family man late for a meeting of the parish council.

"I am very sorry to have kept you waiting so long, gentlemen. This is Detective-Constable Carfax, who will take notes for us, if you can fix him up somewhere."

Broughby fixed him up at the escritoire. Kyle seated himself in a wicker armchair under the high light and was provided with one of the small tables for his notebook and papers. Hardelow and Millard sat on a divan, diagonally facing Kyle. Stranack drew a chair to the side of the divan. Crendon and Broughby took the other divan. There was a short silence.

"I'm ready when you are, gentlemen."

"We haven't appointed a spokesman," said Broughby. "Crendon, would you mind?"

"Not at all, if the Inspector agrees."

Kyle had foreseen this and decided that it would be better to consent.

"Before I attempt to marshal the facts," said Crendon, "I must make it clear that I am not representing this company in any professional sense. I am acting, in an amateur capacity, simply as spokesman—and, of course, as witness. I shall begin by asking Broughby to give his account of how we came to be together on this boat."

# Chapter Nine

Broughby explained that it had been a birthday party for Mabel Rouse, detailed the invitations, then described the cruise to the point where the boat ran into the mud. Hardelow was asked to deal with the mishap—after which Crendon took over and brought the account up to the first incident over lunch. Soup was served, followed by cold chicken, when it was discovered that on the table there was no carving knife. "Carry on, please, Broughby?"

Crendon worked each witness into the narrative and then patted the evidence into place. He soon reached the point where the party was clearing away the lunch and Broughby was taking the crockery basket back to the galley.

"The knife, on top of the contents of the crockery basket, would have been visible to anyone passing down the corridor. Who in fact did pass down that corridor at the relevant times? The answer is that every one of us in turn passed down that corridor—over a period of approximately half an hour. That fact, I imagine, is no more likely to help you to find the murderer than it has helped us."

No one interrupted him while he reported that the first man to go down the corridor was the American, who returned to the saloon about ten minutes later. The second was Hardelow who was absent for a couple of minutes only.

"I was the third to go aft. Before returning to the saloon, I went up on deck and looked about. After a few minutes I rejoined the others. Any comments from those others?"

Broughby looked up.

"I didn't hear your footsteps on deck, Crendon," he said. "And I didn't hear you come down the companion from the deck."

"Did you not? I did go on deck. No doubt the Inspector will investigate the point later. You were the fourth man to leave the saloon, Broughby. Millard was the fifth and—we can say positively—the last. Millard was absent for a long time—I would say about ten minutes, if you all agree."

"I agree that it must have been about ten minutes," said Millard. "But you know why!"

"Just a minute!" Crendon turned to the others. "Has anybody anything to add before Millard takes the floor?"

"I have, though I don't suppose it's important." Broughby again. "When I had put the crockery basket back in the galley, I knocked on Mabel's door to ask if she wanted anything, which she didn't. She did not open the door, but I could tell she was not speaking from the bed."

"She must have opened that door a few seconds later," volunteered Stranack. "It was open when I went down the corridor, and she was on the bed. At her request, I shut it."

"It was shut when I passed by," said Hardelow. Millard said the same.

"And it was shut when I passed it," contributed Crendon. "And now, Millard, will you take on from the moment when you left the saloon."

"On my way down the corridor, I glanced into the galley. I had no conscious purpose and I saw nothing. But I felt uneasy without knowing why—"

"Pardon me, Millard, but wouldn't it be better to leave out what you felt and tell us what you did?"

"No! My feelings—and nothing else—have saved us from the macabre absurdity of taking poor Mabel to Southend regatta." He paused to pick up his thread. "With this feeling of unease I went along and had my wash. On the way back, the same unease made me stop short at the galley. The carving knife was no longer in the crockery basket—on top of the other things—where I had last seen it. That knife had been at the back of my consciousness ever since lunch."

"Why?" interrupted Crendon.

"Because I happened to be watching Mabel's face when Broughby brought it in. She looked frightened and she gave a sort of nod—*at the knife.* You all thought that Mabel was a bit tight. She wasn't! She had two gins before lunch and barely one glass of champagne at table—about half the amount she could carry quite comfortably. She was whipping herself up because she was frightfully upset about something—I don't know what it was. The whipping up didn't work: now and again she looked anxious for a half second or so, and towards the end she became rather noisy and silly."

Prelude to the wedding ring act. Kyle's spirits soared.

"I was as sceptical about my own feelings as any of you would have been," continued Millard. "I searched the galley for that knife. I'm not very good at that sort of thing and I made a lot of noise and broke a plate or two. Broughby heard me and came along. He was not interested—left me in the galley. When I was certain the knife was not there, I made a scene about it in here. You acted promptly, as if you shared my dread."

Crendon resumed charge.

"We thumped at Mabel's door, then tried to open it. Millard, looking through the keyhole, saw only that it contained no key. I took the key from a guest cabin and with it unlocked the door. We saw—what you, Inspector, eventually saw. We did not enter the cabin. We called Broughby."

"Wasn't Mr. Broughby with you?"

"He was not. He did not seem to be impressed by the disappearance of the carving knife." He paused, but without result. "Broughby shut the door, locked it and sealed it with postage stamps. In this saloon we took common counsel, in which Stranack joined. I advised that we should not discuss the case. It was unanimously agreed to make straight for Scotland Yard."

Kyle was pleased. They had obligingly nailed themselves to their tale.

"Let's get this corridor business clear, first!" he said. "Broughby spoke to her through a shut door. Within a minute or so of his going away, she opens the door. It is shut again a few minutes later, by Mr. Stranack, at her request. After that, each one of you passes down the corridor and finds the door shut?"

"That is the evidence of four innocent men," cut in Crendon. "Obviously, the guilty man opened the door, fulfilled his purpose, reversed the key, locked the door and threw the key overboard. Here is your problem, Inspector, in a nutshell. You may safely assume that we are all telling the truth, including the murderer. The murderer is telling lies only in respect of his actions between entering that corridor and emerging from it. I offer you the suggestion—with deference—that the murder was unpremeditated. One of us suddenly saw the tremendous opportunity created by Stranack's presence. One of us must be guilty, but no two of us can be. And the killer believed that the circumstances would make it impossible to prove which one."

Kyle perceived that Crendon was making the mistake, natural to a lawyer, of limiting himself to the facts 'before the court.' He had allowed no margin for discoveries made by the police but not revealed. That wedding ring, for instance, to say nothing of the footprint on the skirt.

The killer was making a similar mistake. The crime was theoretically watertight—a neat little problem turning on the 'insoluble riddle of the door,' as the papers would be sure to call it.

"By your theory, Mr. Crendon, one of you is a maniac, always looking for a safe chance to kill? Or could there be some reasonable motive?"

"There's never a reasonable motive for murder," answered Crendon.

"Oh yes there is!" Hardelow had flared up. "That is, if you think you aren't going to be caught. We can't be cagey, now we're all in this hole. I'm going to blurt out everything about myself and trust to luck. She was sticking me up to finance a play for her—it must be a darned rotten play or they wouldn't have let her hawk it around."

"And she threatened to make certain disclosures if you refused?" asked Kyle.

"Good lord no! She wouldn't do a dirty little crook's trick like that. She thought the play would be a howling success—she always thought everything was going to be splendid."

"Then how was she sticking you up?"

"I dunno! I just felt that if I put up the money I'd be sort of robbing my wife. And if I didn't, I'd be a mean swine. She was that sort of woman. Why, when we hit that mudbank, it flashed into my mind that perhaps poor Mabel would be drowned, and that would be the end of a lot of misery for all of us—except Stranack, of course!"

Kyle made a note that Hardelow admitted motive—then put a query beside it. It was too laboriously frank to be convincing. And how they harped on the impeccability of Stranack!

"As Hardelow has started blurting, we must all follow suit or incur suspicion," said Crendon. "I myself have recently become engaged. I told my fiancée of my friendship with Mabel—and I had no fear whatever that Mabel would do anything unfriendly. But I frankly admit feeling some relief that I can never see her again."

Millard piped up next.

"I was very fond of her, when I didn't want to be. I tried to forget her and was angry with myself when I could not. As she is dead, I am glad she was murdered. It would have been a horrible memory to live with if she had committed suicide—she was so fond of life."

That was a flourish, Kyle told himself. But he remembered that Hardelow, too, had talked mawkishly about the girl.

"I can't quite toe the confessional line!" said Broughby. "This morning I was informed that I had been adopted as Parliamentary candidate. I didn't have to tell Mabel that our menage wouldn't fit in. She told me. In all friendliness and without a thought for herself—without a single stipulation or request—she said she would leave me tomorrow and she meant tomorrow. She was no danger to me. I know she would never have done anything that would injure me."

That would be a reason for taking off the wedding ring tomorrow—not today, in the middle of the party. It was certainly not a reason for flinging it across the cabin. And anyway, the one thing certain about the ring incident was that Broughby was not concerned in it. Looked at from another angle, Broughby's little piece had given the girl another build-up. Possibly this was a technique. The American might be useful here.

"She comes over to me as a very glamorous and fascinating woman," he said. "Mr. Stranack, from what you saw of her, do you agree with that?"

"I would say she was striking looking, not glamorous," answered Stranack, weighing his words. "As to fascination, she was not a clever, mysterious sort of woman. But she had the knack of making a man feel there was something fine in her nature which he had the power to bring out. To put it the other way round, she could draw the ordinary sort of man out of his ordinariness."

Kyle was impressed. He was bound to accept that she was not the ordinary high class joy-girl, but a woman of personality who could produce unexpected reactions. Excluding Stranack, they all seemed to be fond of her and to admire her character, but to wish her dead. You certainly couldn't call that ordinary! Broughby even admired her for consenting to leave him.

"The essential stretch of time," Crendon was saying, "is something less than forty minutes. It begins when Stranack at Mabel's request shut her door. The fact that she was then alive renders Broughby's previous movements unimportant. Thereafter, Hardelow was absent from the saloon for such a short time that I think Broughby will agree with Millard and with me that he can be eliminated. That leaves Broughby, Millard and myself as legitimate suspects."

Kyle had already eliminated Broughby on the ground that he could not conceivably have taken part in the wedding ring act. He now eliminated Millard. From the murderer's point of view, the wedding ring act, involving conversation, would have taken a dangerous amount of time. The murderer would not have wasted more time pretending to look for the knife in the galley—there would have been no sense in it, since it could not create an alibi.

That left Crendon.

"I'll take your layout, Mr. Crendon. You offer me three suspects, including yourself. You yourself obviously eliminate yourself?"

"I do! But that does not mean that I can reasonably suspect an individual—until you have produced evidence of guilt."

The last words sounded very like a challenge. Kyle circled.

"How do you know someone didn't board the boat without any of you hearing him?"

"We must not exclude that possibility!" said Crendon with an air of resolute broadmindedness. "On the land side no one could have approached. On the river side, a skilled waterman, approaching in a small boat, might have succeeded in coming aboard. But with what purpose? Robbery? Mabel had with her in that cabin an emerald brooch and a diamond bracelet—possibly other valuables. Your papers will no doubt corroborate my statement."

Kyle obediently studied the inventory—a painstaking and reliable document, listing every item found in Mabel's cabin. He studied it at some length and then looked up without comment. Crendon continued.

"If we conclude that this hypothetical intruder was not a thief, we have to postulate a maniac, or a disappointed lover. Neither maniae nor lover could have known beforehand that we would run aground there and that these conditions would therefore obtain."

So Crendon was standing pat. No red herrings, even if the police offered 'em. No conspiracy. No means of proving anything against any individual man. Per-*haps!* Kyle got up.

"Excuse me a minute!"

He left the saloon, spoke to his man on guard by the wheelhouse, then came back, sat down and affected to be poring over his notes. In the silence everyone in the saloon heard footsteps on deck. Footsteps of one who walks slowly and self-consciously, as if under instructions from his inspector.

"When Mr. Crendon strolled, as he informed us, on deck, Mr. Broughby did not hear him. Did anyone hear his footsteps?"

There was no answer. Crendon smiled tolerantly.

"D'you know, Inspector, I saw Broughby look at his watch just now. Yet, every fifteen minutes, Big Ben fills this saloon with its din. Broughby heard Big Ben, but he did not notice Big Ben. I repeat, Inspector, that I walked on deck."

"It's only a check-up, Mr. Crendon," said Kyle indifferently, while his thoughts harked back to the wedding ring. Hardelow and Broughby were out of it. He felt compelled to exclude Crendon also. If Crendon had taken part in the wedding ring act and knew that it would be found on the floor, he would have worked it into the narrative, with an answer as glib as the stuff about Big Ben.

That left only Millard. But Millard had wasted time in the galley. Considered as the murderer, he would not have had time for the wedding ring act as well.

There flashed into his mind a suggestion so dangerous to his own position that he felt he must take another look before he leapt. He did a little stage business with his notebook.

"Are you all agreed—" he began slowly. "Are you all agreed that the murder must have been committed before Broughby and Millard met in the galley?"

There were murmurs of assent, which Crendon gathered up.

"After the galley incident, no one entered the corridor until the three of us went to call Mabel."

Kyle nodded. The check-up confirmed his own knowledge of what they had said.

"Can any of you give me a leg-up over this?" He looked from one to another. "We have evidence that deceased talked with someone—probably for several minutes—*after* Mr. Broughby had spoken to her through the closed door."

"You have not forgotten, Inspector," put in Crendon, "that, a minute or so later, the door was open when Mr. Stranack passed, and that he shut it?"

"I was about to say that I had a chat with her, lasting a few minutes." The American, who had been thrust into the role of spectator, roused himself and sat upright in the wicker armchair.

"A few minutes!" echoed Kyle. "How was deceased dressed while you were talking to her, Mr. Stranack?"

"As she was when she was murdered—in her slip."

Kyle concealed his elation by contriving to look shocked.

"I must say, I understood, from the way you gave me the information, that you shut the door in passing?"

"Sorry, Inspector! It didn't occur to me that there was anything to it."

"A few minutes!" Kyle mouthed the words. "You meet her today for the first time. You, as well as the others, give her a good character in spite of her—well—broadmindedness. And there she is holding a conversation with a comparative stranger when she's not dressed?"

Broughby tried to put his oar in.

"Lots of respectable girls, nowadays—"

"We're talking about a particular girl," interrupted Kyle. "Mr. Stranack, did deceased, in your presence, take off her wedding ring and fling it across the room?"

"She did!"

That was good enough for Kyle. There was just one thing that could now make sense of the wedding ring act.

"Was deceased your wife, Mr. Stranack?"

"*Damnation!*" ejaculated Stranack. "Yes, she was! But as it has nothing whatever to do with your investigation, I hoped to keep it off the record."

"Good God, Stranack!" exploded Crendon. "You pulled my leg about her and you treated her here as if you'd never met before."

"I hope you will accept my apology, Crendon, and see it as an innocent deception which could hurt nobody. That still holds good. I apologize to you, too, Broughby. My one purpose was to have a word with her in private, to ask her if she wished to come back to me. I had that word before lunch—and she said she did not want to. So I went on treating her as a stranger.

"When I saw her in the cabin, she told me she had changed her mind, that she was tired of the life she was living and wished to come back to me.

"It was a condition of my offer that she should enable me to pay back any money she had received from her friends, and that she should herself return valuable presents. She referred to this in the cabin. I should explain that she was dramatizing herself a little, though she meant what she said. She there and then removed the jewelry she was actually wearing in the bed and put it under the pillow, assuring me that she intended to return all presents she had received from her lovers at the first opportunity. She took off the wedding ring, which Broughby had given her, and flung it from her with an elaborate gesture and high falutin words to the effect that it held no meaning for her. That is all. I then shut the door."

Another one of the frank, manly confessions that stopped too soon, thought Kyle.

"I take it, Mr. Stranack, that—for the purpose of this conversation—you entered her cabin?"

"No. I remained in the corridor. I had one hand on the door, I think. Probably you've found my prints."

An errant wife accepts an ever-loving husband's offer to take her back, mused Kyle. No kiss! Just a palaver, with him standing in the doorway all the time.

Crendon was looking as if the whole thing were a personal insult. Kyle saw a chance to get a bit of his own back.

"Mr. Crendon, I will not report you to your Benchers if you will give me a bit o' free legal advice. After what Mr. Stranack has told us, is he still so obviously a disinterested person that I can't run you all in for conspiracy?"

Somewhat to Kyle's dismay, Crendon took it as a genuine consultation.

"His membership of the Embassy is now irrelevant to you as a criminal investigator, since there might be a *prima facie* case against him for felony, namely the murder of his wife—alternatively for shielding the murderer of a hypothetically unwanted wife. It is therefore my opinion that, if you were to arrest us all, no action would lie for wrongful arrest."

Kyle felt as if he had fallen over his own feet. Crendon went on:

"But before you proceed to arrest—if that be your intention—I ask you to allow me to make an attempt to clear the matter up? I would add that I personally am sure that my attempt will be successful."

Taking consent for granted, he went behind Kyle's chair, so that he faced everyone in the saloon except Kyle and the shorthand writer.

"I shall not look at any of you, but I want you all to look at me." He fixed his gaze on the copper bowl of flowers on a bracket above Millard's head. "I assert, without proof, that I did not commit this murder. I assert that one of you did. To him I am now speaking."

His tone was even and matter-o'-fact. For the first time, Kyle perceived that the man had dignity behind the bumptiousness.

"On impulse, you killed that dear, delightful, dreadful woman. Why? Because you feared your imagination and your will would never be your own while she was alive. I stand very close to you. When she was mocking my feeling for her by her stupid vulgarity over lunch, I, too, wanted to kill her. You had the courage of your impulse, which I lacked. You relied for your safety—and equally for that of all of us, your friends—on a legal dilemma, which no longer exists. You cannot now wish to ruin us socially and professionally by forcing us to stand with you in the dock—if only for a short time in the lower court. You staked, and you have lost. As your friend I remind you that this is the moment at which you will wish to pay up."

Kyle was almost ready to believe that someone would confess. He glanced at the plaster on Millard's hand. Hardelow sneezed. The moment had passed.

"Thank you, Inspector!" Crendon dropped wearily into the nearest chair. In the silence that followed his appeal, the lines deepened round his mouth so that he looked like an elderly judge at the end of a tiring case.

Millard leant forward on the divan.

"Mabel's legacy!" he cried wildly. "We shall never again trust men of our own kind—nor ourselves. The police will now treat us as the bunch of crooks we have become."

"Well, I must say I'm disappointed," said Kyle. "It couldn't have been put better than Mr. Crendon put it." It occurred to him that the appeal might yet succeed if it were reinforced with a fact or two.

"Before we send for the handcuffs," he grinned, in Millard's direction, "we'll have one more try to get something off the ground."

They were mystified when he stood up, after taking from his bag a ruler and a large safety pin.

"Gentlemen, will you all please come with me to the cabin. Mr. Broughby, can I have two cleaning cloths or two pieces of any soft material?"

In order to produce the cleaning cloths, Broughby headed the procession down the passage.

Kyle broke the police seals on the door. The cabin looked much the same. But the bedding had been removed, revealing a covered spring mattress.

"This plain cloth in my right hand represents deceased's skirt."

He placed it on the floor, by the bed, so that it touched the chalk marking at as many points as possible. "This other, patterned cloth is her jumper—this safety pin stands for the emerald brooch. The position of the jumper is only approximate."

"About ten per cent of it was flopping across the skirt," said Stranack.

"Thank you!" Kyle made the adjustment. "I will now show you all the essential movements of the killer. The movements which we *know* to have been made."

He came out of the cabin, took a few steps in the direction of the kitchen.

"This ruler represents the knife, which he has just taken from the kitchen. I don't know whether the door of the cabin is open—if it is shut, he opens it. But I do know that deceased is not asleep. The killer keeps the knife out of her line of vision—like this, perhaps—because if she were to see it she might scream. She does not see it. She receives him in a friendly manner. He comes in. Sooner or later, he sits on the side of the bed, almost exactly where I am sitting now, his foot on her skirt—like this.

"She puts her right arm round him—whether they actually kiss I don't know. At any rate, he lowers his body in her direction until his left hand can reach her jumper on the floor—like this—without his getting off the bed. He swings the jumper over her head and throat—like this—to protect himself from bloodstains—before he stabs. Whether he was aware of the brooch, again I don't know—he might have caught his hand in the pin—we don't know, yet.

"Then he leaves the cabin, shutting and locking the door, after reversing the key. We assume, with Mr. Crendon, that he then threw the key into the river. Then he returned to the saloon. That's all for now. Thank you, gentlemen."

There was a slow procession back to the saloon, Kyle in the rear. He had shot his bolt, and in the next few minutes would know whether he had hit anything.

"The one among you who is the killer," he said when they were all sitting down, "now knows how much we know."

There should be some sign somewhere, he thought. He glanced at the American who had so readily waived his right to refuse interrogation but was now wearing the traditional poker face.

"Mr. Crendon's very pointed appeal fell flat because the killer still hoped I was bluffing—that I didn't want complications with the Embassy. The Embassy is not my pigeon, I plough on until the higher authorities call me off."

Still the poker face. Come to that, they all had poker faces. His bolt seemed to have missed. He himself no longer believed that was a conspiracy. He accepted Crendon's view that it was a one-man job, with no sympathizers.

He would dodge making a conspiracy charge if he could.

"Mr. Millard, the stain on your trousers is of the same blood group as that of deceased."

"Then so is my own blood. It came from the cut on my hand." He added: "As I told you, it was grazed by the diamonds in Mabel's bracelet."

"How soon after you received the cut did deceased leave the saloon?"

"Broughby brought the plaster. As soon as she had applied it, he grabbed her and took her off. Say a couple of minutes, all told."

"Still wearing the bracelet?"

"Yes—it hadn't been damaged."

"Then microscopic examination of the bracelet should reveal minute pieces of your skin?"

"I suppose so. Hasn't it?"

"We don't know, yet," answered Kyle. Again he turned to the inventory and studied it. Then he decided to take the risk of inventing a spot of science. "In those tests," he asserted, "a lot depends on the nature of the diamonds. What sort of diamonds were they? Where was the bracelet bought, Mr. Broughby?"

Broughby turned to Crendon, who answered:

"I bought it. At Wrenson's. I can assure you they were real diamonds. I gave it to her as a birthday present—with Broughby's consent, of course!"

"That being the case, gentlemen," said Kyle, beaming, "a charge of conspiracy will not be brought. Mr. Crendon, you are under arrest and will be charged with the murder. I assume that the customary caution is unnecessary."

Crendon employed his forensic gesture of non-understanding.

"I am a little dazed, Inspector. You propose to charge me with the murder because I bought the bracelet at Wrenson's?"

"Because the bracelet was on her wrist when she left this saloon for the cabin, because it was seen in the cabin by Mr. Stranack and because it was *not* found in the cabin when we took over. We've never seen that bracelet."

"Therefore the bracelet was taken by the murderer!" said Crendon. "As murderer, I pointlessly take the bracelet and throw it into the river with the key? Or keep it? Really, Inspector!"

"The girl told Mr. Stranack that she intended to give back all the presents she had received from men—at the *first opportunity!* She took off what she was wearing at the time and put it under her pillow."

"Oh, I see!" Crendon's eyes were bright with triumph. "Then, my dear fellow, why on earth didn't you search me before reciting that preposterous formula about charging me with murder?" He stretched out his arms. "Search me now, for heaven's sake, man! Search me, and recover your own sanity!"

"I'd rather you searched yourself, Mr. Crendon."

Crendon's smile vanished. He had been utterly certain that the Inspector would search him—equally certain that he would find nothing. He was still certain that nothing would be found. But his cocksureness had been wiped out by a ford of words.

"That's a damn funny thing for you to say!" he muttered. For a moment, paralyzing doubt held him, while he groped in memory. Then, with a quick, nervous movement, he thrust his hand into his breast pocket.

"Nothing there!" he cried.

"She couldn't reach that pocket. She had her right arm round you while you were sitting on the bed. Try your right-hand side pocket."

With the same quick, nervous movement, Crendon thrust his hand into his right side-pocket and pulled out the diamond bracelet.

He stared at it for several seconds, then laid it on Kyle's table.

"I'm not the only man in this room who was fool enough to think he couldn't live without her. At lunch today she showed me that I couldn't live *with* her—after I had promised to do so." He turned to Kyle, dramatizing himself as deliberately as had Mabel. "Congratulations on your brilliant sequence built on that wedding ring!" On Stranack he bestowed an elaborate glance of compassion. "It's a pity you didn't let me into the secret, old man. Think it over—for the rest of your life.

Lightning Source UK Ltd.
Milton Keynes UK
UKOW03f2124280114

225457UK00002B/13/P